ENCHANTED CHAOS

(ENCHANTED CHAOS SERIES, #1)

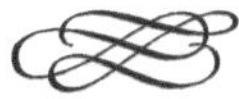

JESSICA SORENSEN

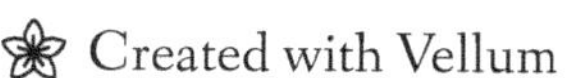 Created with Vellum

CHAPTER 1

I'VE ALWAYS HAD A PRETTY NORMAL LIFE. WELL, except for maybe the fact that my emotions tend to cause ... strange things to happen. Despite that, my life hasn't been too terrible. Is it perfect? No, not at all. But, is anything really perfect?

Still, imperfections and all, saying goodbye to the life I lived for the last seventeen years hasn't been easy. I'm not ready to let go yet, not ready to accept what everyone keeps telling me. That my parents are gone. That no one has a clue as to where they disappeared. That they might not come back.

I've heard rumors around town that they could be dead. That maybe they got into trouble with the wrong people and were murdered. That they over-dosed on drugs. I refuse to accept any of those theories, even though my parents did have a knack for getting in trouble.

They'll be fine. I know they will.

I'm not going to say goodbye yet.

This is only temporary. Your parents will either be found or come back. Don't freak out, Sky.

Just stay calm.

Reach a state of Zen.

If you don't, bad things will happen.

Unfortunately, my friends are freaking out, which is complicating my attempt at reaching a state of Zen.

We're parked at the town park with the windows rolled down, although the temperature is pushing below freezing. But it's either freeze our asses off or let Nina, my best friend since grade school, get grounded for stinking up her mom's car with cigarette smoke. Again.

"This fucking sucks." Nina takes a drag off her cigarette. Wisps of her short, blonde hair blow in her face as she balances the cigarette between her lips while zipping up her jacket. "Can't you just keep living in your house or something? You're a senior in high school, for fuck's sake—you're old enough to take care of yourself."

Gage, my other BFF, rolls his eyes then tugs his beanie lower onto his head. "That's not how it works, hon. They have laws and shit." He leans over the console and steals the cigarette from her.

Gage doesn't consider himself a smoker because he never lights up or buys packs, always bumming off half-lit ones from other people. But if he actually took the time to add up all those half cigarettes he inhales, it'd probably tally up to more than Nina's half a pack a day. Telling him that is a moot point, though.

Gage thinks what he thinks, and there's no changing his mind. I like that about him. He does what he wants, speaks his opinions, and doesn't care what other people think. Part of me wishes I could be like him—more outspoken, bolder, less self-conscious. Unfortunately, I don't usually speak up when I'm surrounded by more than a couple of people. I blame this partly on being an only child. I never really learned how to deal with large groups and the chaos that comes with it. Then again, Nina is an only child, too, and she's about as blunt as they come, so maybe it's just me.

Or maybe it's the fact that being surrounded by people means I have less control over my emotions, which can lead to very bad things.

Very, *very* bad things.

"Maybe if you talk to a lawyer, you can figure out a way to get guardianship of yourself," Nina suggests while restlessly flicking her lighter on and off.

"It's called emancipation." Gage relaxes back in the seat with the cigarette between his fingers. "And Sky might've been able to do that if her parents didn't have a will that gave guardianship over her to someone else. But they do, so ..." He frowns.

The two of them have been bummed out for a few days now, ever since I announced the news that I had to move to another town to live with some family that my dad was apparently close to, although I've never met them.

I'm not thrilled about the relocation, but the lawyer in charge of my parents' will made it pretty clear that I don't have a choice. Even if I did, I can't afford the rent to keep living at my parents' house. So, not only am I moving, but I have to pack up the house and put everything in a storage unit. The real shitty part is my parents have only been missing for a couple of weeks, and I'm supposed to just what? Pack up and move to a town over three hours away? How can I keep searching for them if I'm not here in Honeyton? Plus, this is where I grew up. Honeyton is all I know and leaving it behind is freaking me out. But, in typical Skylin fashion, I've kept a lot of my worry bottled up.

My mom used to tell me, if I didn't stop doing that, one day I was going to have a panic attack. I wanted to tell her that, if I ever did have one, the whole town might ignite in to flames. But, since she isn't aware of my supernatural ability that is attached to my emotions, I've always kept my lips zipped.

"Her parents haven't even been found dead yet," Nina grumbles as she reaches for her pack of cigarettes on the dashboard. Then she suddenly pauses, her worried gaze flicking to me. "Sky, I'm so fucking sorry. That was totally insensitive."

I zip up my leather jacket and prop my boots up on the dash, remaining calm. Because calm is easier than actually feeling what I feel. "You're fine." I hug my arms around myself as the winter air seeps into my bones. "My parents aren't dead, just missing. I tried to point that out to the lawyer, but he said I didn't have a choice. My parents have a will, and that will states that, until I'm eighteen, if anything should happen to them, I have to go live with these Everettson people." I rest my head against the headrest and take a deep breath to steady my heart rate. "What I don't get is why they put these people on the will when I've never even met them before."

Gage inhales from the cigarette. "Aren't you related to them?"

I shake my head. "No. The father is supposedly my dad's best friend. But, how can they be that great of friends if I've never even heard of him?"

It's been bugging me since the lawyer told me. Why would my parents decide to leave me with people I don't know? Then again, the only remaining relative still alive is my mom's sister, who I haven't ever met. From what I understand, she currently lives at some mountain retreat with a bunch of middle-aged, free-spirited people who believe in a simplistic life-style. When my mom told me this, I stated that it sounded an awful lot like a cult. She only laughed and patted my head, saying, "One day, you'll understand why not everyone wants to live in this modern day, technology-driven world." Maybe she was right, but right now, I can't even imagine parting with my cell phone or laptop.

"Don't you have someone you're related to that you can go live with?" Gage asks, flicking the cigarette out the window.

I shut my eyes, the chilly air burning my lungs, but inside, I feel a hot spark in the center of my chest.

Shit.

Calm the fuck down, Sky.

I gradually exhale. "Just my aunt. But I... I don't even know how to get a hold of her or I would've tried already." I would've tried the day I realized my parents weren't coming back from the bar.

They had told me they were going to go out for a while to get a couple of drinks at the bar a few blocks down from our neighborhood. That was nothing new.

My parents usually spent Saturday nights drinking there with their friends.

They left around nine o'clock at night, and I fell asleep around midnight. When I woke up around ten the next morning, their bed was empty and still made, which I thought was odd but not completely out of the ordinary. There had been a couple of times when they'd gotten too drunk and passed out at a friend's house. And sometimes they'd take off for a few days to go on road trips, but they usually checked in when they did that.

Around three o'clock on Monday, after two days of not hearing from them, I started making calls to everyone I could think of. No one had seen them since early Saturday morning. Not even at the bar.

When I realized they'd never made it to the bar, I panicked, which led to a fire erupting in the middle of the living room. After I put it out, I took a few shots of vodka to calm the hell down. Then I called the police.

It was another twenty-four hours, three exploding light bulbs, and two small fires before I could fill out a police report. My emotions had been all over the place that night, along with my ability. In fact, I hadn't felt so out of control since I was six years old and discovered my emotions set off elemental-related reactions—fire, wind, water, ice, etc.

No one knows about my ability, not even my friends.

If someone did find out, I might end up becoming a lab rat for scientific experiments or be put into a psych ward, which is part of the reason I'm so worried about moving in with a strange family. The change might disrupt my emotions too much ... and my ability right along with it.

But the only way I can get out of moving in with them is if my parents just simply return home or the police find them. The latter seems unlikely since, so far, the police have only asked around town and did a quick search through the house. None of the evidence they found indicated any signs of foul play.

I overheard an officer telling another officer that he thought my parents had just bailed on me. When I told him he was wrong, he looked at me with pity and said, "Kid, as much as I hate to say this, you might not know your parents as well as you think you do. A lot of kids don't."

I got what he was saying, but that doesn't mean I believe him. Sure, I live on the other side of the railroad tracks, the lower-class area of Honeyton where the drug and crime rates are higher, but that doesn't mean my parents would just bail on me.

They're decent enough parents. They have jobs. They put a roof over my head and food on the table. And yeah, they aren't home a lot, but they'd never just leave me.

Knowing that doesn't make me feel any better, though, because it means something bad has more than likely happened to them.

I suck in a breath as tears sting my eyes and ice begins to spiderweb across the windshield.

Crap. I need to calm down.

Calm down, Sky. Calm down now!

I inhale another deep breath, then another, and the ice crackling finally ceases.

"Earth to Sky." Gage waves his hand in front of my face.

I tense, worried he noticed the ice on the windshield. "Yeah?"

"You seriously spaced out for, like, five minutes straight."

"Sorry," I apologize, breathing in relief. "I was just thinking about stuff."

Gage and Nina trade a concerned look, and then Nina's gaze zeroes in on me. "You know what I think we need?"

"A time machine so I can fast-forward six months into the future to when I turn eighteen?" I crack a joke.

She cranks up the defroster. "Nope. Although, that'd be awesome."

"Yes, it would." I straighten in the seat and lower

my feet to the floorboard, watching the ice on the windshield melt away. "So, what do we need?"

She gives me a sly smile. "What's the one thing that you've been wanting to do but have never had the balls to go through with?"

As I figure out what she means, I hastily shake my head. "Nope, not going to do it."

"Aw, come on, Sky." She taps the steering wheel with her palm. "This might be your last chance."

"Yeah, the last chance to humiliate myself." The last thing I need right now is to set off my emotions.

She steers onto the icy road and toward the center of town. "You won't know that until you try."

"I may not know how it'll go down, but I have a pretty good idea of how it'll end." I roll up my window and recline back in my seat. "With me talking to him and then looking like a loser when he laughs in my face."

She pops the end of a cigarette into her mouth and signals for me to light it for her. "Dude, Grey so messed up your head."

I pick up the lighter and flick it on. "This isn't about Grey." That might be a lie.

Truthfully, I'm not sure if I'm just shy around guys or if Grey's overdramatic rejection of my dance invite —Nina's idea, not mine—in eighth grade permanently dented my self-esteem. And when I say overdramatic rejection, I mean he turned me down for the dance by standing up on the lunchroom table in front of the entire eighth grade and announced it to everyone. Even worse, I reacted by crying, which resulted in the pipes bursting and the entire school flooding.

Yeah, thanks for that, Grey.

Still, I can't blame my lack of a dating life completely on him.

Dating sometimes leads to falling for someone, which can lead to heartbreak which, in my case, can then lead to what I can only guess would be flashfloods and wildfires. I mean, look at what happened with Grey. I barely knew him at the time and his rejection caused my ability to flood the entire school.

Of course, it doesn't help that after Grey turned me down, he's spent years relentlessly tormenting me, along with his friends. While I try to avoid him as much as possible and he generally doesn't bother me when I'm around Nina and Gage, there have been a couple of incidents where he's tormented me to the point where I've lost control over my ability and disaster soon followed.

As for the guy Nina wants me to talk to right now, I'm unsure if he's an asshole or a nice guy, since I know nothing about him, not even his name or if he even lives in Honeyton. The only thing I do know is he visits the auto shop on the corner of Main Center

Street and Winter Mourning Road every Friday evening around four o'clock, right when I'm heading home from school. I'm not certain what he does there or how long he stays there, just that he goes there. That's it. Well, that and he's extremely good-looking and mysterious, but the latter might only be because of my lack of information on him.

"You know Grey's a jerk, right? He's a cocky, arrogant douchebag who loves to humiliate women." She inhales then exhales a cloud of smoke. "Do you know how many times I've heard him putting down a girl or slut-shaming them? He's probably done it to at least half the girls in our school."

I tuck a strand of hair behind my ear. "I already told you this isn't about Grey."

She removes the cigarette from her lips and gives me a disbelieving look. "Do you understand, though, that Grey's just an ass? Because, if you did understand that, I think you'd be more willing to do this."

Gage squeezes my shoulder. "Don't listen to her. If you don't want to do it, don't." He reclines back in the seat. "Don't let her use her peer pressure bullshit on you."

She throws him a glare from over her shoulder. "I'm not trying to peer pressure her. I just think talking to this guy might be easier for her if she understands that she'll never have to see him again. And it might help her get over her fear of rejection." She looks at me. "But, if you don't want to, just tell me to shut the fuck up."

"Shut the fuck up," I say with a small smile. Deep down, I know she has a point.

Ever since the fiasco with Grey, I've been afraid and have never dated anyone. I've never even kissed a guy.

Besides, I could use the distraction from the constant worrying of where the hell my parents are. And the emotions attached to that worry. As long as I don't panic while talking to this guy, everything should be okay. What would I even have to panic about? Nina is right. I'll never see him again.

"You know what? Let's do it." I glance at the clock. "If we leave now, we should get there right as he's showing up."

"Really?" Nina perks up.

I nod. "Yeah, really."

"Awesome." Grinning, she steers the car toward the shop.

I grin back, but my stomach kickflips. God, I really hope I can keep my shit together for this.

CHAPTER 2

"Maybe this was a stupid idea," I mutter as Nina pulls into the auto body shop's parking lot a couple of spaces away from his 1968 Chevelle.

Usually, I only see the mysterious stranger when we're driving home from school. The first time I spotted him was a couple of months ago when I was walking home. Nina had been sick that day, and Gage had afterschool detention.

The distance from my school to home is about five miles, and I had decided to trek on foot instead of suffering through a bus ride and dealing with the mess of emotions that comes with that. I don't mind walking, but I'd worn uncomfortable shoes that day and was cursing my decision. But then I had spotted the mystery guy and was sort of glad I had opted to walk, even if my boots were dirty, evil bastards that made my feet bleed.

As a fan of classic cars, his vehicle was what drew my attention first. But then he had climbed out of the car, and I immediately became distracted by him.

Tall and lean with short, dark hair, he wore all black, a chain dangled from his belt loop, and he had a couple of tattoos inked on his arms. Even from afar, I could tell he was good-looking, but that wasn't what made me keep watching him.

It was the way he rounded to the back of his car, leaned against the trunk, and lowered his head into his hands, as if he was crying. I started to feel awful for him.

I might have stuck around and struck up a conversation to see if he was okay, if Grey hadn't driven by and shouted something foul at me.

After that, I hightailed my ass home.

I thought I'd never see the stranger again, but then, the next Friday, his car was parked at the auto body shop again.

It became like clockwork after that. Every single Friday, his car is at the shop and sometimes he's standing out by it. I don't know who he is or why he goes there. While he looks around my age, he doesn't go to my school, so he either graduated already, dropped out, or he lives somewhere else.

"You need to throw up before you do this?" Nina asks as she shuts off the engine. "You look pale as shit."

"Shit's not pale." I grin nervously as I sit up straight in the seat and peer out the window at his car, trying to keep a grasp on my nervousness. *He's just a guy. Chill out, Sky. You're never going to see him after this.* "He's not even out here."

Nina reaches for her phone. "So, we wait then."

"Doesn't that seem sort of stalker-ish?" I flip down the visor and examine my reflection.

My long, wavy brown hair is swept messily to the side and looks like I just ran a mile in a windstorm. My kohl eyeliner is smudged, and my lips are chapped. Where my makeup is minimal, my piercings stand out; a stud above my lip and a series of earrings trim my ears. My outfit consists of a leather jacket, a plaid shirt over a black shirt, and torn jeans tucked into a pair of clunky boots. Nothing that screams, *hey, look how sexy I am.* Then again, dressing up has never been my style. I like grungier, edgy clothes, and usually wear dark colors.

"You look great," Nina assures me. "You always do."

"I look like a hot mess, but thanks for saying that." I flip up the visor and crinkle my nose as a thought occurs to me. "What if he's short?" My long legs put me taller than the average guy, and since I prefer a guy taller than me, it makes finding one difficult. Not that I've tried. "I mean, I've seen him from a distance, and he seems like he's not. But, what if I get out and he's like only up to here?" I hold my hand flat below my chin.

"Then I guess ..." She trails off as her gaze drifts out the windshield. "Well, if that's him, then I don't think the short thing is going to be a problem."

I track her gaze to the mysterious guy I've been obsessed with for the last couple of months. He's standing beside his car with his attention fixed on his phone, and when my eyes settle on him, the sky grumbles with thunder.

Calm down. He's just a guy.

"That's him, right?" Nina asks, glancing at me.

I nod, my pulse accelerating. This is as close as I've been to him, and I realize he's better looking than I thought. Too good looking.

Way out of my league.

Another boom of thunder that matches the quickening of my heart.

Shit, this was a really bad idea. I need to get out of here.

"I changed my mind." I reach to refasten the seatbelt. "I can't do this."

"Oh, come on, Sky," Nina gripes. "We drove all the way over here."

"From two miles away," I gulp as the auto body shop sign flashes on and off.

"Yeah? So? It was still out of our way." She turns to me with a stern look on her face. "You've been obsessed with this guy for months now, and this might be your last chance to talk to him."

"You act like I'm never coming back to Honeyton." I swallow down a shaky breath. "This move ... it's only temporary. As soon as my parents are found, I'm coming back. And I plan on visiting you guys, and I was hoping you'd visit me. I don't—can't lose you two. Not with everything going on ..." Tears burn my eyes, but I suck them back.

Chill out. Breathe.

Her expression softens. "I know." She grips the steering wheel. "Fuck, I'm the shittiest friend ever."

"No, you're not," I assure her. "In fact, you might be one of the best."

She slightly relaxes. "Yeah?"

I nod. "Yeah."

"I'm trying not to feel left out here," Gage remarks from the back seat, "but what about me?"

I smile at him. "You're pretty awesome, too."

He smiles but then frowns. "You know we're going

to visit you, right? We won't let you go through this alone."

"Plus, you have all the good shoes, so I'll have to visit at least to borrow them," Nina jokes, but her eyes start to tear up. "I'm really going to miss your jokes and shitty pep talks."

"And I'm really going to miss your bitchiness and dirty jokes." Tears flood my eyes, and even though I try to fight them back, a few escape down my cheeks.

When rain begins drizzling from the sky, I curse my ability. Seriously, it's bad enough just to have a strange, supernatural ability, let alone one that's like a surprise grab bag. I never know what's going to happen with it, whether my tears will cause floods, rainstorms, fires, or electricity to go haywire. If I could just figure out why I have the ability to begin with, perhaps it wouldn't be too terrible. But I've tried countless times to find info on it with absolutely zero results.

As rain trickles from the clouds, the mysterious stranger glances up at the sky. His brows knit before he goes back to staring at his phone, letting the rain drip down on him.

Nina traces her fingers underneath her watery eyes. "I don't want to say goodbye."

"Me neither." I blink back the tears and exhale slowly. And just like that, the rain stops.

The moment is pretty heavy for Nina and I—like me, she keeps emotions bottled up a lot—so when Gage sniffles in the back seat, we both seize the distraction.

"Aw, look, we broke Gage," Nina teases with a wicked grin.

He turns his head, discreetly wiping his eyes. "You didn't break me. I have something in my eye."

She snorts a laugh. "Okay." But her laughter fades as she looks back at me. "Look, if you don't want to talk to this guy, then say the word and I'll leave, okay? But I just have to say one final thing first." She holds up a finger. "You've been scared of guys forever, but this can be your chance to get over that fear." She nods at the guy. "You're probably never going to see him again. Whatever happens, good or bad, is going to end here. He won't be able to pull a Grey on you. He's not going to humiliate you at school." Her hand falls to her lap. "You're never going to get good at talking to guys until you start actually talking to them. That's generally how things work in life."

I let her words sink. She has a point. This issue I have with guys—with people in general—is always going to remain unless I rip off the Band-Aid and learn how to keep my shit together while I'm around others. I've done it with Nina and Gage for years now. Perhaps it's time to branch out. And what better way to start than to strike up a conversation with a guy who I'll never see again? It can be like practice.

"You know, for someone who can't make up their mind about anything, you're awfully good at helping others do it." Blowing out a breath, I reach for the door handle.

She perks up. "So, you're gonna do it?"

My palms are so fucking sweaty. "Yeah, I'm going to do it."

Grinning, she reaches for her pack of cigarettes. "Damn, I'm good. I really should start charging an advice fee or something."

Rolling my eyes, I push open the door, then pause. "Wait. What should I say to him?"

She shrugs as she lights up. "Just tell him he has a nice ass or something."

Gage rolls his eyes. "So much for giving good advice."

Nina narrows her eyes at him. "If you're so smart, then what's your advice?"

Gage lifts his shoulders. "Just talk to him about his car."

I raise my brows. "His car?"

Gage shrugs again then steals Nina's cigarette. "He drives a Chevelle and spends a hell of a lot of time at an auto body shop. Clearly, he's into them."

"But I'm not a car expert," I point out as I lower my feet onto the puddled asphalt.

"Yeah, but you like classic cars, enough to know a little bit about them, right?" A cloud of smoke circles his face as he exhales a drag from the cigarette.

So much for not stinking up Nina's mom's car.

"I guess." I peek up at the sky and the sign to make sure everything seems calm at the moment. When no rainstorms, electrical shortages, or random flames are evident, I climb out.

As I make my way toward him, he doesn't look up from his phone, so he doesn't notice me coming. Probably a good thing since I can barely keep a rein on my nerves.

Just breathe. You got this.

I take an uneven inhale as I reach him. "Nice car."

He looks up and his gaze scrolls across my body and face. He has these crazy blue eyes. Mine are blue too, but his shade of blue is more vibrant, almost other-worldly, and reminds me of a cloudless sky.

"Thanks." He reverts his attention to his phone.

As impending rejection begins to sting, the puddles below me ripple. I inhale and exhale, then press on for God knows what reason. Probably sheer stupidity.

"What year is it?" I ask, even though I know the answer.

He sighs, clearly annoyed. "A '68."

I open my mouth to ask questions about the engine, but he cuts me off.

"Look, whatever you think is going to happen here, isn't. I'm not interested. And I'm not going to be interested, no matter what you say. So, quit wasting my time and yours." He stuffs his phone into his pocket then hops into his car.

Humiliation burns underneath my skin and ripples through my body, powerful, potent, sharp. While I'm use to the feeling, of rejection, his hurts worse, the sting potently piercing—

A lightning bolt snaps down from the sky and zaps the auto body shop sign, sending sparks shooting everywhere.

The guy glances up with his brows crinkling, glancing from the sign to me. My eyes widen then I reel around and jog back to the car without so much as glancing back.

"Holy shit, did you see that?" Gage's wide-eyed gaze is fixed on the low, lightless sign.

I nod, shutting the door. "The damn rainstorms here are crazy sometimes." I play it off the best I can, but holy crap, this is bad.

"Fuck the lightning." Nina stares at me worriedly. "What happened with him?"

I shrug, sinking lower into the seat, forcing myself

to stay composed and refusing to look over at the mysterious stranger. *No more losing control.* "Nothing, other than what I thought would."

"Sky ..." Nina says with pity.

"Can we just go?" I beg as I buckle my seatbelt. "It's our last night to hang out together, and I'd rather do something fun than obsess about that asshole. Plus, the storm's getting pretty intense."

As if responding to my words, the wind kicks up, sending leaves scurrying through the air.

Nina glances up at the greying sky then drives forward onto the street.

The three of us remain silent for the next few minutes until Gage finally breaks the silence.

"Sky, you're a beautiful girl, whether you believe so or not." He places a hand on my shoulder. "Guys are just assholes sometimes."

I force a tiny smile. "Thanks for not falling into your gender stereotype."

"And just remember, you never have to see that jerk again," Nina adds in an attempt to cheer me up.

The reminder does make me feel better. Unlike with Grey, the embarrassing encounter will never get thrown in my face again. I can just move on.

Move on, Sky, move on.

If only things were that easy. But moving on is

never easy. Life isn't easy. And the rain pouring from the darkening sky reminds me of that.

Not wanting to be a downer, I do what I've been doing for the last two weeks. I plaster on a fake, shiny smile and pretend everything is okay. Maybe if I keep pretending long enough, I'll start believing it myself, and then the rain, fires, and electricity will finally go away.

CHAPTER 3

Darkness circles me, wrapping around me like snakes. I can't breathe. Can't think. I need to get free, need to protect myself.

I dig deep inside me, for the first time ever, begging for my powers to manifest.

Lightning flashes above me and fizzles across my skin, as the wind kicks up, sending darkness swirling through the air. A fire ignites from somewhere. Ice crackles. And then the mysterious stranger appears in the center of the chaos—

Knock. Knock. Knock.

KNOCK. KNOCK. KNOCK.

The obnoxious noise pulls me from my trippy dream.

"Oh, my God, what the hell is that?" Gage groans from beside my feet.

After the whole disaster with the mysterious stranger yesterday, we decided to spend the night at my house and have one final hurrah before my new guardian shows up to drag me away. I was nervous for half the night as the wind continued to howl and rain flooded the streets, but then Nina got a bottle of whiskey out from my parents' stash and one thing led to another, and then ... Well, let's just say I passed out right about when Gage started throwing up.

KNOCK. KNOCK. KNOCK.

I try to force my eyelids open, but my entire body feels heavy. "I have no idea what that noise is," I mutter. "But maybe, if we ignore it, it'll self-destruct."

"If it doesn't self-destruct soon, I'm going to destroy it myself," Nina grumbles. "It's making my fucking head hurt."

"You should stop talking. It'll help with the noise a bit." Gage rolls onto his side and accidentally kicks me in the shoulder.

Why his feet are so close to my face is beyond me. Then again, I'm unsure what room we're even in. Or house. For all I know, I could be lying in a car right now.

"Shut the fuck up, Gage," Nina growls.

"Make me," Gage quips through a yawn.

"Guys, I'm too tired and hungover to listen to you two bitch," I intervene before their fight escalates.

KNOCK. KNOCK. KNOCK.

"For the love of all sanity," Nina whines, "Sky, please make that noise stop."

Sighing, I pry my eyelids open and take in my surroundings. Relief washes over me that I'm not in the car but lying on the sofa in my living room. Gage is curled up at my feet like a cat with one leg stretched out across me, and Nina is sprawled out on the floor with a mountain of throw pillows surrounding her, along with a half-empty bottle of whiskey and several boxes. The place is a mess, but at least we went out with a bang.

I smile a little at that. But it's a bittersweet smile.

KNOCK. KNOCK. KNOCK.

My gaze darts to the door where the annoying noise is coming from there.

I pick up my phone from off the table to check the time.

"Shit. That's probably that Mr. Everettson dude," I mumble as I stumble to my feet.

Combing my hair out of my face, I trip around the mess of pillows, pizza boxes, and the empty beer bottles that I don't even remember drinking and throw open the door. Then I instantly cringe.

Standing on the other side is a tall, middle-aged

man with short brown hair, a scruffy beard, and crazy silver eyes. He has on a T-shirt, worn jeans, and worker boots, looking as though he's about to go to work at a construction site. But that's not what has me cringing.

The front yard is covered with fallen tree branches and the grass is so soaked it looks like a swamp. The street isn't any better. Tree branches and large puddles cover the asphalt.

Lovely, Sky. You destroyed every tree within a mile radius.

"Skylin?" the guy asks with hesitancy.

Tearing my gaze away from the street, I blink at him. "Yeah."

A smile breaks out across his face. "I'm Gabe Everettson. It's so nice to finally meet you." His smile slightly fades. "Although, I wish it were under better circumstances."

A beat of silence passes. My head pounds, and my throat is as dry as my frizzy hair. I want to tell him to leave, that I'm fine living here on my own. That I'm fine.

Fine. Fine. Fine.

Maybe if I repeat the word in my head enough times, it'll actually come true.

The sky grumbles as if warning me that I need to at least pretend to be fine.

He studies me with his lips pressed together. "Look, we don't know each other, and I can only guess how hard this must be for you, but I promise my family and I are going to do everything in our power to make sure you feel comfortable living with us." He massages the back of his neck while muttering, "I owe your father that much. Maybe even more."

My brows dip. "Owe him for what?"

He drops his hand to his side as a drop of worry flickers in his expression. "For saving my life once."

My brows rise toward my hairline. "My dad saved your life?"

He nods. "He never told you the story?"

I shake my head. "Honestly, up until my parents' lawyer read the will, I didn't know you existed. Or that my parents even had a lawyer. Or a will." My parents have never been the type to plan for the future. Or, at least I thought so. I guess I was wrong.

Maybe that officer was right. Maybe I don't know my parents as well as I thought.

I hastily shove the thought from my mind. No, I knew—know them. They wouldn't just take off and leave me on my own. At least not for this long.

"Yeah, your father and I sort of drifted apart after college," Gabe explains. "But, up until then, we were pretty close. And he did save my life once. If you want, I can tell you the story sometime."

I smash my lips together and nod. "All right."

"Good." He claps his hands together, matching the clapping of thunder. Then his gaze wanders over my shoulder. "Let me get my sons, and then you can show us what you're taking with you and what we're putting in storage, okay?" He turns to walk away.

"Wait ... Sons?" My gaze flicks to the truck and trailer parked in the driveway where I can make out two figures inside, one in the back seat and one in the front, but the windows are too tinted to make out faces and ages. "You have kids?"

He stops at the bottom of the stairs and faces me. "Six actually. Six sons. But don't worry; they're not too scary." He smiles, but it looks a bit forced.

Lovely. He's afraid of his own kids.

Being the only child, the idea of living in a house with *six* other kids, not to mention all guys, just seems straight-up crazy. And emotionally challenging.

"Do they all live with you?"

He nods. "My youngest are seventeen, and my oldest is twenty-one and in college, but he hasn't wanted to move out. Hunter and Holden are in college, too, though Max, the second oldest, isn't. But they all still haven't moved out yet. I blame my wife. She spoils them all too much." He laughs it off, but again, a hint of nervousness edges into his expression.

Considering I have plans with Nina and Gage to

move out the moment we graduate and then travel, the idea that even one of his kids wants to stick around after they turn eighteen is mind-boggling. Don't get me wrong; my parents aren't terrible, but I've been taking care of myself since I was old enough to work the stove, so moving out of the house won't be that much different. Nina is the same way. Gage, too. We've practically run wild since we were kids, which is fine—I enjoyed the freedom, for the most part anyway. It's part of the reason I am so agitated that I can't live on my own now.

I can take care of myself. My parents know this. Yet, they decided that, until I'm eighteen, I can't live on my own? That living with some strange family will be better?

I don't want to live with strangers. What I want is for this unsettling feeling of unknowingness that's been plaguing me to go away.

I stare at the road, as if expecting my dad's truck to suddenly appear. It doesn't. But a lamppost flickers on and off.

Blinking a few times, I focus back on Gabe. "How old are your other kids?"

He actually has to think about it. Really, I guess I can't blame him. He has six kids for crying out loud! He probably has a hard time keeping track of them all.

"Porter is twenty-one, Max is twenty, Holden and

Hunter are nineteen ..." When I pull a funny face, he adds, "They are twins. Identical, too. Can be sort of a problem telling them apart sometimes, but the trick is to never refer to them by their names. That way, they don't know when you've confused them." His eyes glint with humor. "I'm just kidding. Holden actually has a small scar above his right brow. And I brought Easton and Foster with me. They're the youngest and twins, too. Not identical, though. And they're seniors, like you, so they should be able to show you around school and stuff."

"You have *two* sets of twins?"

He nods then steps forward to pat my shoulder. "I know it's a lot to take in, but trust me; after a while, you'll get used to it."

I bob my head up and down, kind of in shock. Six kids. Two sets of twins. That's eight people in one house. Nine counting me! *Jesus, how big is his house?*

"All right."

He points a finger at me. "You're kind of a quiet one, aren't you?"

I shrug. "Not always, but sometimes." Around people I don't know.

"Well, I don't want to frighten you"—he backs for the porch steps again—"but you might want to consider being a little more outspoken, or the chaos of the Everettson family is going to swallow you up." He smiles then turns around, leaving me with a huge lump of fear wedged in my throat.

Might want to be more outspoken? Yeah, every time I've tried that, I ended up humiliated.

Zap. The lamppost on the street sparks.

Dammit. I'm already an emotional wreck. Makes me worry how the day's going to end.

As he jogs back to his truck and opens the passenger side door, I step inside and attempt to collect myself. I'm still wearing the plaid shirt and T-shirt I had on yesterday but traded out the jeans for a pair of cut-offs sometime during last night's drunkenness. I smell like beer, whiskey, and stale pizza, just like this living room. Hopefully, Gabe doesn't have issues with the mess or the evidence that I was drinking last night. My parents never cared, just as long as I never drove drunk or got arrested.

Gage sits up on the sofa and rubs his bloodshot eyes. "Who was that?"

I pick up the half-empty bottle of whiskey from off the floor. "Gabe. My … temporary guardian, I guess."

Nina buries her face in a pillow. "Did you tell him to go away?"

"I wish I could." I rotate the bottle in my hand as an unspoken silence blankets over us. "God, I can't believe this is really happening."

"Me neither." Nina sniffles then staggers to her

feet and wraps her arms around me. "You have to come back every weekend, and we'll drive out there when you can't come here. And promise that none of our plans will change. We're still moving in together after we graduate, okay?"

I nod, giving her an awkward hug back. "Nothing's going to change. I promise." But I feel like such a liar. Because things are changing.

Everything is changing.

Too quickly.

And I can barely keep up.

As tears threaten to pour out, I start to pull back when Nina abruptly stiffens.

A jolt of static currents through my body. Why are my powers going off right now? I'm fairly collected...

"What the fuck are you doing here?" She crosses her arms as she glares at someone behind me.

"Who are you talking to?" I ask, twisting around.

Then my heart slams against my chest and another burst of static hums through me.

No. No, no, no, no, no. This can't be happening.

I blink. Then I blink again. I blink so many times my eyes begin to water. Yet, the guy standing in the doorway remains.

The mysterious guy I tried to hit on yesterday.

He appears as stupidly dumbstruck as I do—his eyes wide, his expression frozen.

Well, at least he remembers me.

Yeah, remembers how he told you to get lost.

Wait. Do I smell smoke?

I peer around, silently demanding my anger and embarrassment to simmer down. Luckily, no flames are anywhere, but I still need to get my emotions under grasps.

"So, what are we moving out first?" A guy around my age suddenly steps through the doorway with a smile on his face. He's dressed similar to the mysterious stranger—all in black—but instead of short, dark hair, his hair is chin-length and blond. He also has silvery eyes like Gabe. When he enters, he takes one look at me, Nina, and who I'm assuming is his brother, then frowns. "Aw, hell, Foster. Please don't tell me you've already fooled around with our new sister?"

The shock that had swept across the room rapidly thaws.

"I'm not your sister," I say while the mysterious stranger—Foster—bites out, "I didn't mess around with her, and you know that, asshole." Then his gaze zeroes in on me and his jaw ticks. "And even if I could, she's not might fucking type."

My jaw nearly drops.

What a fucking asshole.

The blond guy openly checks me out. "Maybe... She's definitely my type, but I'm not really interested either."

Now my jaw nearly ninja-kicks the floor.

Great, they're both assholes. The only difference is Blondie does it with a smile on his face, while Foster just seems irritated. Well, that and I feel more hurt about Foster's rejection. Who the heck knows why. After yesterday, I should be over him—I need to get over him.

My insides coil as Blondie's smirk widens. Then the floor quivers, just slightly, but no one appears to notice. If I don't get my emotions under control, I may start an earthquake. Luckily, Gabe strolls in and deflates the situation with a clap of his hands.

"Have we done introductions yet?" When he notices Nina and Gage, his asks me, "Are these your friends?"

I nod, continuing to glare at Blondie. "Yeah, they stayed over last night to say goodbye."

Gabe's attention drops to the whiskey bottle in my hand, and a frown etches into his face. "I see."

Great. Am I in trouble?

Blondie smirks at me while Foster stares at me with his brows arched.

"Well," Gabe starts, shaking the frown away. "How about we get this little moving fest going so we can get you home and let you know all the house rules, okay?"

Awesome. My bet? Rule number one is no drinking.

Gabe starts to walk across the room but then pauses, turning toward Foster and Blondie. "Did you guys introduce yourselves yet?" When they shake their heads, seeming bored, he sighs. "Skylin, this is my son Easton"—he gestures at Blondie who has the audacity to wink at me, then motions to Foster—"and this is Foster."

So, these are the non-identical twins who are my age and who are supposed to show me around my new school. *Lovely.*

I force a smile. "My name's Sky. No one really

calls me Skylin, except for my mom, and only when she's really pissed off."

Gabe smiles at that, Foster continues to look irritated, and Easton, well, he looks amused, but I have a feeling that might not be a good thing.

"Okay, Sky it is," Gabe interrupts the silence, seeming a bit uneasy as he looks at me. "Why don't you show me everything that needs to go with you, and then what needs to go in storage. That way, we can load up the storage stuff last so we won't have to move all your stuff around.

Nodding, I turn for my parents' bedroom, figuring that's the best place to start. As I pass by Nina, I hand her the whiskey bottle and tell Gage and her to wait a minute before taking off.

After I get done showing Gabe what goes where, he suggests the strangest thing.

"Why don't you go have lunch with your friends and say goodbye," he says. "Foster, Easton, and I can handle getting everything packed and cleaned up."

I peer around the messy house crammed with furniture. "Are you sure? There's a lot of stuff."

He pats me on the shoulder. "With everything you're going through right now, you deserve to say a proper goodbye to your friends."

I nod gratefully, but a drop of uneasiness stirs inside of me.

He acts as though I'm saying goodbye forever, as if he knows my parents are never coming back. But even if my parents don't return—and that's a huge if—I'll eventually come back to Nina and Gage. My time with the Everettsons is only temporary. I know this, so why doesn't Gabe not seem to?

CHAPTER 5

BEFORE I LEAVE THE HOUSE WITH NINA AND GAGE to grab a bite to eat, I change out of my smelly clothes, wash my face, comb my hair, and put on the necklace I almost always wear. It was a gift from my mom on my fifth birthday. She told me her sister had once given it to her.

The teardrop-shaped pendant is made out of steel and is supposed to bring the wearer good luck. But, considering how unlucky I've been, I don't buy into the story.

After I get cleaned up, I head out. Easton makes a point to smirk at me again, and Foster simply ignores me.

"Well, they're an ... interesting family," Gage

comments from the back seat of Nina's car as we drive toward the center of town.

"Interesting?" Nina glances at him in the rearview mirror. "They're a bunch of assholes."

"Gabe doesn't seem too bad," I attempt to find the silver lining in all this.

Maybe the rest of the family will be like Gabe? I sure hope so, or else my time with the Everettsons is going to be all rain clouds, fires, and sporadic lightning zaps.

"Yeah, except for the fact that he looked upset you were holding a bottle of whiskey," Nina reminds me as she pulls into the parking lot of the local burger joint.

"So, he's a normal parent then," Gage chimes in with a shrug. "That might not be that bad."

"Have you ever had a normal parent?" Nina questions, knowing very well he hasn't. "Because my ex-stepfather was like that—all about rules and normalcy—and it sucked ass." She steers into an empty parking space then unbuckles her seatbelt. "I was so glad when my mom divorced him and things went back to normal."

"And by normal, she means she got to return to her evil vixen ways of running wild, drinking, and doing drugs." Gage shares a teasing smile with me as he slides across the seat to get out.

Laughing, I climb out of the car and meet Nina and Gage around back.

"I still can't believe you're going to be living with the guy you've been crushing on for the last couple months," Nina says as we head inside.

"*Was* crushing on," I clarify, splashing through puddles. "The crush ended the moment he opened his mouth."

"Well, asshole or not, at least you'll have something pretty to look at every day," Nina muses. "That Easton guy was pretty hot, too."

"They're twins," I tell her as I pull open the door.

She grins as she steps inside. "Even better."

Gage and I share an amused look as we follow her in.

"You know she's going to hit on him at least one time, right?" he whispers to me as we wander toward the counter.

"As long as she comes and visits me, I don't really care," I whisper back.

"Are you two bitches talking about me?" Nina grins. "It's cool if you are. Just make sure it's all good things."

A smile touches my lips. Man, I'm going to miss this—miss them. Even on the shittiest days, the two of them can make me smile.

The smile remains on my face as I skim the

choices on the menu. I'm dithering back and forth between a hamburger and chicken tenders when Gage lets out a sharp cough.

"Creeper alert at five o'clock," he hisses under his breath.

I casually tilt my head, glancing to my right to see what Gage is yammering about. Standing a little ways to the side of us is a tall man, maybe a few years older than us, with dark eyes and black hair that reaches his chin. He has a scar across his forehead, a series of unrecognizable star patterned symbols branding his neck, and strangely, he is wearing slacks and a button-down shirt with the sleeves rolled up and the top button undone. Even businessowners in Honeyton rarely sport suit attire, so he stands out like a ballerina in a mosh pit. What really makes him creepy, though, is the way he's staring at me, as if he's attempting to burn a hole into my head with mind powers or something.

"Do you know him?" Nina glances from the stranger to me.

I shake my head and start to look away when the stranger approaches us. I tense as he nears us, wishing I brought my pepper spray.

"You're that girl moving in with the Everettsons, right?" His voice is shockingly deep.

I feign stupidity because there is no way in hell I'm about to tell him the truth. "Who?"

"Don't lie to me, little girl," he warns, a bit of an accent seeping into his tone. "I know you're moving in with them. I came here to warn you to be careful." He looks at my friends and then leans in and lowers his voice. "They're not who you think they are."

"I have no idea who you're talking about." I resist the urge to gulp as my pulse accelerates and the lights above me flicker on and off.

The stranger glances upward then back at me. He stares at me confusedly as he reaches into his jacket pocket.

Fearing what he could possibly be grabbing, I instinctively step back. But he only retrieves a card.

"When you want to find out the truth, call me." He urges me to take the card.

I keep my hands at my sides. "Look, I don't know who you are, but I'm not sure what you're talking about …"

He drops the card at my feet, spins on his heels, and then strides out the door, glancing at me one final time before walking outside.

"Holy hell," Nina breathes out. "That was beyond creepy."

"Agreed." Gage bends over and picks up the card. "Okay, this just got even creepier."

"What?" I take the card from him, and my brows knit. "It's blank."

"Yeah, I know." Gage scratches his head. "That was really strange, especially how he knew you were moving in with the Everettsons." He looks at me with worry. "Do you think we should call the police and report him?"

"It wouldn't do any good. Technically, he didn't break a law. And considering how interested the police have been in finding my parents, who are *missing*, yeah, I don't see the point in telling them." I restlessly pat the card against the palm of my hand.

While the entire ordeal with the man was bizarre, the strangest part was when he glanced up at the lights then at me when I made them flicker, as if he knew about my strange ability.

But, how could he possibly know about that when I've never told anyone? How did he know I was moving in with the Everettsons? And what did he mean by the Everettsons aren't who I think they are? I'm not sure, but the whole ordeal has me on edge and really wishing for my parents to return.

CHAPTER 6

An hour later, Nina pulls up in front of my house to drop me off. We spend about fifteen minutes hugging and saying goodbye while promising to visit each other every weekend. Then as I'm getting out of the car, they give me a goodbye gift.

"Because I have a feeling you're going to need it," Gage explains as I glance in the gift bag that is full of an assortment of mini bottles he must have stolen from his mom, along with a small, wooden box. "There're a couple of joints in that box, in the false bottom. I'd recommend keeping them in there, too, until you're ready to light up." His gaze travels to the Everettsons' truck in the driveway. "That Gabe guy seemed like he could be pretty strict."

"Yeah, it's definitely going to be interesting living with him." I hug the gift bag against my chest.

"The gifts are from me, too." Nina rummages around in her purse. "But I also got you this." She hands me a small box.

I lift the lid and smile at the gift inside—a silver lighter with my name engraved on it. It's totally a Nina type of gift.

"Thanks, guys."

We sit there silently for a moment and everyone's eyes begin to water. I should get out of the car. I *need* to get out of the car before my waterworks gets the best of me and the clouds begin to cry as well, ruining all my stuff piled in the back of the Everettsons' truck. But getting out means it's time to go.

It's time to go, Sky. Get out of the car.

Sucking back tears, I push open the door.

"Best friends forever!" Nina shouts.

We used to say that all the time when we were kids.

"Best friends forever," I repeat then shut the door and walk away, making my way across the grass and toward my house.

Walking away from my old life and toward my new.

"About damn time," Easton says as I wander through the front door and into the living room.

He's sitting on the floor, resting back on his hands, with a soda bottle beside him. He's the only thing in the room, the furniture and boxes now gone.

"You guys got everything out of the living room already?" I ask in surprise.

"And the rest of the house." The corners of his lips tug into a smirk. "We've just been waiting around for your slow ass to get back so we can hit the road."

"But I was only gone for a little over an hour?" I shake my head. No, there's no way they could've cleared out the house already. He has to be screwing with me.

I march back to the bedrooms to check for myself with Easton's snickers chasing after me. As I stick my head in one room after another, I start to wonder if maybe Easton was telling the truth. When I reach the final room—the washroom—I find the answer.

That room, like all the others, has been cleared out.

Confusion tap dances in my head.

How on earth did they get everything out so quickly? Sure, they're three decently sized guys, but my parents had a lot of stuff crammed into the house, along with a few huge pieces of furniture. With how small of a trailer Gabe brought, I thought we were going to have to make a couple of trips to get everything in storage

"Oh, good, you're back," Gabe greets me with a smile as I return to the living room.

Easton is still stretched out across the floor, and Foster is leaning against the front doorjamb with his arms crossed. The door is open, and his gaze is fixed on the street outside.

"You got everything loaded up already?" I ask the obvious, still a bit skeptical. "I didn't think it was all going to fit on the trailer."

"We actually already made one trip to the storage unit," Gabe explains, taking a sip from a water bottle. "We just need to drop the last load off, and then we can go. I thought, if you were ready, we could lock up and drop the keys off at the landlord's on our way." He twists the lid back on the bottle. "Of course, that's only if you're ready. If you want to stay here for a little bit while we drop off the last load and say goodbye, I completely understand."

My gaze skims the bare, patched-up walls, the stained carpet, and the empty space around me. Say goodbye to what? This place is no longer my home anymore. It's just a house. That's it.

I don't have a home anymore.

Don't have a family.

I smash my lips together, battling down my emotions as thunder rumbles outside.

"We better get going soon. It looks like it's going to

storm again," Gabe mumbles with his forehead creased. "Although, the forecast said it was supposed to be sunny all day." He looks at me. "So, did you want to stick around here for a bit and say goodbye?"

Bottling down the pain, I shake my head. "Nah, I'm good. There's nothing left to say goodbye to anyway."

I turn and walk out of the house that was once my home. Walk away from everything I've ever known and toward the frightening unknown.

CHAPTER 7

AFTER WE LEAVE, WE STOP BY THE LANDLORD'S house to drop off the key then we head over to the storage unit. During the drive there, I remain stuck in my thoughts of how the life I once knew is no more. But the instant we pull up to the storage unit, my thoughts shift back to how quickly the guys moved my stuff out of the house. One hour. That's how long it took for them to clear out a three-bedroom house and the attic. And that includes driving to and from the storage unit ten miles away.

Something doesn't add up. Did they maybe have other people come over and help? If so, why didn't they say something?

They're not who you think they are, the stranger's words echo in my mind.

Who the hell do I think they are? Because I sure as heck don't know.

"So, are you this quiet all the time?" Easton asks from the passenger seat after his dad climbs out to unlock the storage unit.

Foster is sitting in the back seat with me and has been silently staring out the window the entire drive.

I shrug.

He studies me with a glint in his eyes. "Well, just a warning. Being quiet at our house means being eaten alive."

I pick at my fingernails. "Yeah, your dad already warned me about that."

"Did he?" Easton grins at Foster. "What do you think about that, Fost? Sounds like Dad is trying to play favorite with our new little sis."

"Please don't refer to me as your little sister," I say. "This situation is only temporary. The moment my parents are found, I'm moving back to Honeyton."

"And what if they're never found?" Easton asks with his brow cocked. "Then what, little sis?"

"I'm not your little sis." I twist toward the window as I mutter, "And if, for some crazy reason, my parents aren't ever found, I'm taking off the moment I graduate and never looking back."

"Sounds like a great idea," Foster mutters. "Maybe you should take off now. Easton and I have some money we can give you, if you can't afford your own place."

I breathe in and out, my fingers curling into fists, and stabbing my fingernails into my palms in an attempt to keep my emotions under control—physical pain over emotional pain always seems to affect my powers less. "That's a great idea, and one I'd love to do, but since my parents left my guardianship rights to your father, I'll be considered a runaway if I try to take off before I turn eighteen."

I catch Foster's reflection in the window as he shares a look with Easton.

"What if we could help you disappear?" Easton suggests. "We're really good at that."

I slowly turn my head and measure them up. Easton's lips are curled into a grin, while Foster has a frown etched onto his face.

"Is that an offer?" I glance between them. "Or a threat? Because, if it's a threat, you should know that I have a can of pepper spray in my pocket that I've used more than a handful of times, and I'd love to use it again. Practice makes perfect, right?"

Easton sinks his teeth into his bottom lip as his gaze glides to Foster. "I don't know, Fost," he says with amusement. "She might just fit in with us after all."

Foster's narrowed eyes bore into me as he shakes

his head. "No way. She'll never fit in. Newbies never do."

I raise my brow. "Newbies? How many people have you guys had live with you?"

"You're the first person we've ever had come live with us," Easton replies with hilarity.

Foster shoots him a dirty look, to which Easton's smile magnifies.

"You're walking on thin ice, East," Foster warns. "Be careful."

More than done with their cryptic conversation, I push open the door.

"Hey, where are you going?" Easton calls out with laughter ringing in his tone.

"To help your dad unload the truck." I start to shut the door when anger waves over me and, I add, "And to get away from your stupid asses."

As I slam the door, a cluster of lightning bolts illuminate across the sky, bright enough to burn my eyes and make my heart jump.

"Wow," Gabe mutters from near the back end of the truck with his head angled up toward the sky. "I've never seen anything like that before."

"Me neither," I divulge truthfully.

I may have spent years setting off crazy lightning storms, floods, and windstorms, but never have I seen anything quite like what just occurred in the stormy grey sky. Makes me wonder how upset I truly am at the moment.

Makes me worry what sort of disasters I might set off the longer I'm around Foster and Easton.

CHAPTER 8

I help Gabe unload the truck to the best of my ability, but eventually, Foster and Easton get out and take over. It takes us a while to get everything unloaded, and Easton and Foster start to complain about how slow I'm moving, as if all this is my fault. Technically, I guess it is, considering they're only here because of my parents' will. Still, it's annoying. They're annoying. This entire situation is annoying.

By the time we're finished and climbing back into the truck, I'm bursting with annoyance and the sky is more than reacting, raining hail down upon the earth.

"Man, this is some shitty weather," Gabe remarks after we all hop into the truck. He turns on the engine then flips the wipers on. "We're lucky we're done."

Foster nods in agreement as he fastens his seatbelt. "What do you think's causing it?"

I find his question somewhat strange, unless he's some sort of science person and is asking his dad to literally explain what causes hailstorms.

His dad shrugs, worry creasing his face as he peers up the sky. "I'm sure it's just a ... cold front or something."

Okay, so he did mean it in the literal sense.

A bit of relief washes over me. I'm not even sure why. It's not like any of them could possibly know about my ability.

"Yeah, I guess it is December, isn't it?" Foster mutters, seeming perplexed.

What a weirdo. He acts as if hail in December is some rare occurrence when it's not. Not really anyway. At least not when I'm around.

"We should stop by Nelly's on our way home," Easton suggests as Gabe steers the truck forward and out onto the road. "We haven't seen her in forever, and I need to talk to her about some stuff."

"You can text her then," Gabe says, his gaze fleetingly straying toward me before returning to the road. "We really just need to get home."

"Texting is so overrated." Easton groans dramatically. "And I'd rather not have every goddamn thing I say recorded into the system." He flops back in the seat. "Some conversations are private, for fuck's sake."

System? Wait ... Is he one of those people who believe the government is secretly spying on us through technology?

"Watch what you say," Gabe warns, giving Easton a pressing look.

Easton rolls his eyes. "Fine, Pops, I'll chill for now. But eventually, you're going to have to let us be us or shit's going to get complicated."

Gabe rubs his lips together, clutching the steering wheel. "I know."

The cab grows quiet after that, tension lacing the air.

I'm not really sure what to make of their cryptic conversation ... If it has anything to do with me or not.

Just exactly who are the Everettsons? That's quickly becoming the million-dollar question, isn't it?

Well, that and a hundred other things.

CHAPTER 9

No one says much for the rest of the drive, and by the time we reach the Everettsons' house, the hail has toned down a bit. Of course, the moment Gabe pulls up in front of the massive, three-story home, my pulse quickens with anxiety and the sky ignites in response.

"Damn this weather," Gabe says as rain drizzles from the clouds. "Hopefully, it'll ease up a bit before tomorrow's ... tournament."

"Shit, I didn't even think about that." Easton shoves the door open to get out. "What'll we do if it rains?"

"Still have it probably." Gabe starts to get out but pauses, glancing at me. "Our family participates in baseball tournaments every Sunday."

Unsure why he's telling me this, I nod. "Sounds cool."

He offers me a stiff smile. "We'll be gone all day, which means you'll get the house to yourself."

That thought sounds nice, although I feel a bit hurt he didn't invite me to go. Then again, I'm not part of their family. Just some strange girl they got stuck with. I'm not even sure if my dad talked to Gabe before he listed him in their will to be my guardian.

What if he didn't? What if all Gabe's tense smiles are because I'm not really wanted here. Foster and Easton don't seem too thrilled about my presence. Maybe that's how the entire family feels.

Forcing a smile, I say, "Okay."

His lips part, appearing as though he wants to say more, but then he gets out of the car.

Easton and Foster follow without saying a word, and none of them wait for me as they start up the paved walkway that leads to the double-doored, column-lined entrance of the colossal house.

Sucking in a breath, I steady my nerves and climb out of the truck. My boots splash in the puddles as I trail behind them, taking in the massive house, the spacious yard, and the five-car garage. I can't even wrap my head around how big and fancy this place is, and it leaves me feeling confused.

How does my dad know someone who can afford a

place like this? As far as I know, he grew up living in poverty in Honeyton.

I really need to talk to Gabe and hear the story, but maybe after a few days when I've gotten settled and used to the idea of all this.

"I hope Charlotte made dinner already," Easton announces as he pushes open the front doors. "Moving shit makes me hungry."

"It's not even five o'clock," Foster says as he steps inside. "It's not going to be ready yet."

"I can request an early dinner," Gabe tells them. "Just let me check in with your mom first and see if she's okay with it."

"Who's Charlotte?" I find myself asking as I step inside and take everything in.

Holy shit, this place is huge, with a high, peaked ceiling, a wide staircase, black and white tiled floors, and the glitteriest chandeliers I've ever seen—maybe the only chandeliers I've ever seen.

I'm never going to feel comfortable here.

"She's our cook and housekeeper," Gabe tells me. "If you need anything to eat at all, you can ask her."

Yeah, I'm not sure I feel comfortable with that.

"Can I just make my own food?" I ask, feeling very uncomfortable at the moment.

Is this how I'm going to feel every day?

Gabe gives me a strange, concerned look. "You're

more than welcome to if you want, but just know the option is there."

I force yet another strained smile. "Thanks."

His smile mirrors mine but morphs into a real one when a woman with flowing blonde hair appears at the top of the stairway.

She looks around the same age as my mom, but that's about where the similarities stop. Where my mom is all torn jeans and leather jackets with wild curls, this woman is sporting a flawless white pencil dress, matching heels, and a string of pearls decorates her neck.

"That took you longer than I thought." She starts down the stairway, each of her steps graceful.

Her words make no sense at all. How could she think we'd be back sooner when I'm not even sure how the guys managed to move everything so quickly?

"The weather slowed us down a bit." Gabe meets her at the bottom of the stairway and places a kiss on her cheek.

The scene makes me miss my parents even more than I already do, and thunder booms in response.

"Was it storming over in Honeyton all day?" the woman wonders while smoothing Gabe's hair into place. "Because it's been great weather here up until now."

"It rained almost the entire time we were there,"

Gabe says, his gaze traveling to me. "It looked like a pretty bad storm blew through last night, too?"

I nod, even though I'm not sure if he's directly asking me. "It storms there a lot."

I'm not sure what the big deal is. So it's storming? It's freakin' December and totally normal. Sure, I know the real reason behind the storms, but they don't.

Before he can say anything more, the woman's weird but beautiful shade of lavender eyes light up. "Oh, my gosh, you look just like your parents." She swings around Gabe and puts a hand on each of my arms, her gaze scrolling over me before zeroing in on my eyes. "And those eyes ... Jesus, they're gorgeous... You look just like her."

Two things puzzle me about her statement. 1). My eyes are far from gorgeous, the color is just a simple blue. Well, a bright blue, but still, blue eyes are really common. And 2). I don't look very much like my parents, both of them having blonde hair and green eyes.

She must read the confusion on my face because she adds, "I met your aunt Aurora a couple of times, and she looks a lot like you."

"You've met my aunt?" Hurt stabs my chest. *I haven't even met her.*

"It was a very long time ago," she explains, smoothing my hair away from my face, acting very motherly. "As far as I know, she hasn't had any contact with the real world in ages."

"My parents haven't spoken to her in years." I pause, deliberating my next words carefully. "They've also never mentioned you guys."

"We've seen each other a couple of times over the years, but we haven't been close since college. I wish that had never turned into the case, though." She sighs sadly. "I was so upset when I heard what happened to them."

"So, you know my parents, too?" I ask, and she nods but makes no effort to embellish. "Who are you exactly?" I'm assuming she's Gabe's wife, but she hasn't introduced herself, so I'm not positive.

"Oh, my goodness, I completely forgot to introduce myself, didn't I?" She laughs then steps back and sticks out her hand. "I'm Emaline, Gabe's wife and the mother to the six hellions who live in this household."

"It's nice to meet you." I mean my words. Emaline seems nice enough.

We shake hands, and then she casts a quick glance at Foster and Easton. "I hope everyone's treated you wonderfully today."

Easton and Foster smile at their mom, but then Easton smirks at me when she turns back around. Foster's smile dissipates, too, as he gives me a hard look. It almost makes me want to tell Emaline the truth, but I also don't want to deal with drama, so …

"Everyone's been awesome," I lie with a plastic smile.

She visibly relaxes while Easton's smirk magnifies and Foster rolls his eyes.

"That's great to hear. I was a bit worried …" She shakes her head and smiles at me. "Would you like to see your room? I'm sure you've had an exhausting day and probably need a bit of a break from the chaos."

I nod, more than eager to lock myself up in a bedroom where I can pretend this isn't my life now.

Pretend.

Pretend.

Pretend.

"Great." She turns to Easton. "Do you mind showing her to her room while I go make sure Charlotte is getting everything ready for tonight's dinner?"

An exaggerated smile takes over Easton's face. "Of course, Ma."

"Thank you, sweet boy." She ruffles his hair like he's still a little kid then heads off toward a door located on the far back wall.

"I'm going to get started on bringing in your stuff," Gabe tells me. Then he pulls open the door and steps outside, leaving me standing in the foyer with Easton and Foster.

That stupid smirk instantly consumes Easton's face. "Come on, Fost; let's go show lightning eyes her new room."

Great. He's given me a nickname.

Foster rolls his eyes. "Mom said you had to do it, not me."

"Trust me; you're going to want to be a part of this." His smile makes a chill trickle down my spine.

And that chill only grows colder as a small smile touches Foster's lips.

"Fine." Foster starts toward the stairway.

Easton follows him, motioning for me to come on. But I hesitate. When he notices my lollygagging, he sighs.

"Hurry your ass up, lightning eyes," he says. "We've already wasted half the day taking care of you."

Foul words tickle at the tip of my tongue, but I bite them back and trail after them as they walk up the stairway. When we reach the top, they lead me down a hallway lined with closed doors. The deep blue walls are decorated with family portraits, and the light from outside filters in from the occasional skylight. The farther I get into the house, the more in awe I become. It's so big and nice and lavish and completely the opposite of what I'm used to, but not in a good way.

I want to go home.

Tear sting my eyes, but I force them back as we stop in front of a shut door at the end of the hallway.

"Welcome to your new home." Foster grins as he twists the knob and shoves open the door.

My stomach instantly drops at the sight of an old, rickety stairway on the other side.

"Well, aren't you going to go in?" Easton asks when I make no effort to step over the threshold.

Wrapping my arms around myself, I summon a breath and step inside, staring up at the top of the stairs. The lights are off, so I can't see where they lead to, but cobwebs line the railing.

Are they being serious or just messing with me?

"There's a bed up there and a dresser." Foster slants against the doorframe with his arms crossed. "Our house is already full, so this is the best my parents can do. You can either take it or leave and go live somewhere else."

My fingernails stab into my palms as I battle not to lose control of my anger. "I already told you that I can't leave."

Mustering up every ounce of strength I have left, I start up the stairs, telling myself that maybe it's not as bad as I think it's going to be. That the stairway is just a dusty mess because who cleans stairways anyway? But then I reach the top step and realize how wrong I am.

Honestly, I probably wouldn't have been able to see anything if, at that precise moment, lightning hadn't zapped across the sky. With all the skylights on the roof, the entire room lights up with a bright blue glow, giving me a brief glimpse of the dusty floorboards, the unfinished walls, and the twin bed perched in the corner.

A thunder boom of a second later, a light flips on above my head.

"The light switch is down here," Easton calls up the stairway with a snicker. "Enjoy your new home, lightning eyes." At that, a door slams shut.

Part of me worries maybe they locked me in, but at this point, I don't think I care. Not when I'm on the verge of crying.

A wave of sadness rolls over me as I inch farther into the room, the floorboards creaking beneath my feet. Part of me really wants to believe this isn't my room, that Easton and Foster are screwing with me, but then I note the fresh blankets on the bed and the clean pillows. Someone has made a bit of an effort to clean this up, for my arrival, I'm sure.

Sighing, I walk over to the bed and sit down, looking around. The only other items occupying the space is a dresser, a lamp, and a wooden trunk. Curious, I get back up and try to open it, but it's padlocked shut.

Weird ...

Why put it up here in my room if it's locked?

Scratching my head, I move back to the bed, lie down, and stare up at the windows above me. Rain sprinkles across the glass in light drizzles, lightning occasionally flashing and thunder booming. The longer I lie there, the more tears threaten to pour from my eyes, and the more the rain increases. When a sob manages to escape my throat, thunder rumbles so hard the entire house shakes. Something about the movement unleashes a pain from inside me.

I start to cry uncontrollably, the sound louder than even the hail clinking against the glass. I try to get myself to stop, knowing the streets are going to flood if I don't, but I can't seem to find the willpower I used to possess.

CHAPTER 10

Somehow during the mad chaos of hail and
tears, I manage to doze off. When I wake up, the entire
space is dark and quiet, the thunder and lightning
gone.

Blinking dazedly, I peer around, attempting to get
my bearings. I can't see a damn thing, other than a bit
of moonlight trickling through the windows. That's
when I realize the storm toned down during my nap,
but that's not too uncommon. Night has also fallen
while I was out, leaving me to wonder what time it is.

Rolling over, I dig my phone out of my pocket, and
a drop of light trickles through the darkness as I swipe
my finger across the screen. Shit, it's ten thirty, which
means I've been asleep for over six hours and missed

dinner. With how quiet the house is, I'm betting every-one's gone to bed already.

What doesn't make sense, though, is why my bedroom light is off. Did someone come up here when I was asleep? I'm not sure how I feel about that ... No, actually I do. I feel really, really uncomfortable. In fact, this entire day has been nothing but a series of uncomfortable occurrences.

Maybe I should just go back to sleep and pretend I'm someplace else until tomorrow morning ...

My stomach grumbles in protest, reminding me that I've barely eaten all day.

"Fuck, I need to eat something," I mutter, rolling out of bed.

Turning on my flashlight app, I make my way across the room and down the stairs. Then I try to turn on the light, but it doesn't come on. Great, the power's out.

Beaming my phone around, I glance around at the cobwebs covering everything. Thankfully, I can't see any spiders or else I'd be running out of here screaming.

Sucking in a shaky breath, I reach for the door-knob, crossing my fingers I'll be able to find the kitchen on my own so I can at least grab a snack and some water. But I freeze right before I pull the door open as voices flow in from the other side.

"Sky, are you sure you don't want anything for dinner?" Emaline asks over the sound of a knock.

The strange thing is, the knock isn't on my door.

I start to open my mouth to reply to her when I hear Easton say, "She was acting really weird when we showed her to her room."

"She would barely talk to us," Foster chimes in. "I think she might just want to be left alone."

"She's probably so terrified," Emaline mutters. "I can only imagine what the poor girl is going through."

"I bet she wants some time to herself," Easton tells her. "I know I would if I was in her situation."

"I agree with East," Foster says.

A beat of silence trickles between them.

"What did you guys do?" Emaline asks suspiciously.

"Nothing," Easton and Foster say simultaneously.

Emaline heaves an exhausted sigh. "I'm going to try to find your father. Maybe he can talk Skylin into coming out of her room, if nothing else, at least to eat something."

Silence lingers in the air for a moment, and then an unfamiliar deep voice asks, "All right, what did you two assholes do?"

"Nothing," Easton says. "We did nothing at all."

I hear a *whack* and then an, "Ow, fuck, that hurt."

"Yeah, well, it's going to hurt a lot worse if you

don't fess up and tell me what you did to Skylin," the deep voice says.

"Whatever, Max," Easton grumbles. "We didn't do anything to her, other than make sure she stays out of everyone's way."

"Which needs to happen," Foster emphasizes. "You know it does."

"Maybe," the stranger—Max—mutters in agreement. A long pause passes between them, and then he sighs. "Look, I know this situation is complicated but, for whatever reason, Mom and Dad seem pretty set on taking this girl in. And we need to respect that and trust they'll keep our secrets protected."

I slant back from the door. *Secrets? What secrets?*

"Mom and Dad aren't thinking clearly," Easton points out. "All they care about is that they owe Skylin's parents. They're not considering what it's going to be like for all of us having her live under the same roof." He spits out the word *her* as if it's vile—as if *I'm* vile.

"I'm sure they considered it and figured we were smart enough to be able to keep our shit under control." A warning rings in Max's tone. "So, we better make sure that happens, got it?"

"Whatever," Easton mutters. "I can't make any promises."

"Just tell me where she is," Max says tiredly.

"Because I know she's not in the room Mom's been knocking on."

Silence skips between them.

"We may or may not have put her in the attic," Easton admits with a surprising hint of guilt in his tone.

"With my *trunk*," Max hisses, and then the doorknob in front of me begins to twist.

I step back as the door swings open and a guy who looks a couple of years older than me appears in the doorway. Max, I'm assuming.

From what Gabe told me earlier, Max is twenty years old and the second to oldest. He's also not a twin, although he looks a lot like Easton, only his chin-length hair is black. And like Easton and Foster, he's sporting all black attire, except for a grey shirt. He also has leather bands on his wrists and a couple of intricate tattoos weaving up his forearms that create strange symbols and markings.

I wonder what they mean ...

His vibrant green eyes widen when he spots me, and then he nearly trips over his feet. "Hey ..." He looks me over, question marks flooding his eyes. "Okay, you so weren't what I was expecting." He glances at his brothers with his brow arched, not saying anything, just staring them down.

Strangely, Easton and Foster both squirm, something I didn't think could be possible with how arrogant they both are.

"We told you she has eyes like lightning." Easton shrugs as if this answers whatever silent question Max is asking.

When Max continues to stare him down, I smile to myself as Easton gets all squirmy. When Foster notices my grin, his lips curve upward, but then they hastily falter.

What is with this guy? And what secrets was Easton talking about? And what the fuck is in that trunk?

So many questions dance around in my mind, but evaporate as Max offers me a charming smile.

"You must be Skylin." He sticks out his hand. "I'm Max. I'm the second to oldest in the fucking litter that is my family."

"I know. Your dad told me who everyone was." I eyeball his hand dubiously.

After the shit that's gone on with Easton and Foster, I'm reluctant to shake it. Perhaps he's going to pretend to be nice only so he can push me back and lock me up in the attic. Which, from what I just overheard, I'm guessing isn't really where I'm supposed to be staying.

"It's okay. I promise I don't bite." He holds back an amused smile as he urges me to take his hand.

Still a bit hesitant, I slip my hand in his. "It's nice to meet you," I mutter.

He smiles, but a crinkle forms between his brows as he holds my hand. "You're like a blank canvas," he mumbles confusedly. "I can't read you at all."

"Max thinks he's a people reader," Easton clarifies, nudging Max in the side. "*Thinks* being the key word."

Max winces, but then his lips tilt into a smile. "Sorry about that," he apologizes then reluctantly releases my hand. "I'm not really good with intro-ductions. "

"Me either." My gaze skims the three of them, their rigid posture and the smirks are no longer evident on Easton's and Foster's faces. In fact, they're all staring at me curiously.

Oh, now I'm a curiosity, huh? What happened to hating me?

Something feels off ...

"But anyway." Max clears his throat, causing Easton and Foster to look away from me. "I'm not sure what my brothers told you, but this"—he points up at the stairs behind me—"isn't your new room." He steps toward me, and I have to tilt my head up to meet his gaze. Good God, I'm tall, yet he makes me feel short. "I'm sorry for whatever they said or did to you. I'd like to say this isn't how they normally act, but that'd be a huge fucking lie."

"Oh, shut the hell up, Max," Easton says with an eye roll. "Don't pretend like you haven't ever pulled a prank on a newbie."

"Newbie?" I question. "You guys keep saying that ... Easton said you don't take a lot of people in, though ..." I trail off, so lost.

"People?" Max muses with a genuine smile. "No, we really don't."

What a weirdo. Granted, a hot weirdo, but still ...

Easton and Foster are hot, too, and if I've learned anything from them today, it's to never trust a hot Everettson. Honestly, at this point, I'm starting to believe maybe I shouldn't trust hot guys in general, considering my track record with them.

Max grins, watching me with interest. "Your confusion's adorable."

Easton lightly smacks his shoulder and hisses, "Dude, Mom said not to hit on her."

He was hitting on me? I nearly snort a laugh. Yeah right.

But when Max continues to stare at me without protesting, I wonder if maybe he is. The question is: why?

Wait. Maybe this is a prank?

"Yeah? So? Mom's not here, is she?" Max says to Easton without taking his eyes off me. "And if you don't tell her about this, then I'll make sure not to tell her that you two jackasses told this pretty girl that the attic was her bedroom." He glances at something above my head, then a frown forms on his face as he reaches over and flips the light switch off then on again. When not a drop of light flows around the room, his frown deepens. "Were you stuck up there with the power off?"

"I wasn't stuck up here. I could've walked out at any time," I point out. "And the lights were on when I fell asleep, but when I woke up, they were off." I shrug. "I just figured maybe someone turned them off."

"The storm probably tripped the breaker." Max turns to Easton and Foster and smacks them on top of their heads. "Fucking hell. What is wrong with you two? Making her sit up there in that dusty piece of shit room in the dark? Do you know what could've happened if it found…?" He trails off, gulping.

Easton swallows audibly. "I'm sorry. But in our defense, we didn't realize the power went off."

Foster yanks his fingers through his hair, his gaze flitting from me to Max. "It was just a prank, okay? We didn't mean for the damn power to go off."

"A prank that could've gone very wrong," Max says in a low tone, tension flowing off him.

"What's going on?" I eye them over skeptically. "Do you guys have a bat locked up in the attic or something?" I stiffen, realizing that could very well be it.

"Or something," Max murmurs. Then he wiggles his shoulders, clearing the tension, and turns back toward me, pointing to the shut door to the side of him. "This right here is your room. Would you like to see it? I promise it's way better than the attic."

With everything that's happened over the last handful of hours, I'm not sure if I trust him. Sure, he seems nice enough, albeit a bit weird. Then again, so am I …

What do I really have to lose at this point? Besides, anything's better than sleeping in an attic, right?

I sure hope so.

I will my lips to turn upward. "Sure."

He smiles then offers me his hand.

Seriously, he wants me to take his hand? Half of me really wants to, mainly for the sole reason that I've never held a guy's hand, let alone a guy this gorgeous. But the other half of me worries this is all a prank.

"Relax. I already said I'm not going to bite," Max assures me then slips his fingers through mine and tugs me down the last step.

Easton and Foster trade a look, and then Easton rolls his eyes.

Max ignores them, steering me in front of the shut

door. I reach for the doorknob with my free hand, but Max stops me, placing his hand over mine.

"Before you go in," he says, "I want to ask, if you could have your dream room, what would it look like?"

I shrug. "I don't know. I've never really thought about it."

He wets his pierced lips with his tongue, amusement dancing in his eyes. "Humor me, okay, and just try to picture it."

I cast a sidelong glance at Easton and Foster and find their eyes hold the same amusement.

Great. This has to be a prank.

For a flash of a second, an image of my dream room materializes in my mind. Black and purple walls, a massive four-poster bed enclosed by curtains, a gothic chandelier, and a couple of dressers.

"What does it look like?" Max asks, observing me curiously.

"I don't know," I lie, not wanting to give them any sort of ammunition. "I like purple and black, so maybe something with those colors." I leave it at that.

"Really?" A smile lights up Max's face. "That's so weird, because everything in this room is pretty much black or purple." He pushes open the door and gestures for me to look.

As I tentatively step in, I half-expect the room to be painted in bright-ass orange or something, but nope.

Almost everything from the walls to the bed to the chandelier is either a deep purple or a shimmering black. The room is huge, too; almost as big as my old living room and bedroom combined.

"Wow," I mutter as I turn in a circle, taking in the lavender curtains enclosing the bed and the ebony ceiling that shimmers like stars. "This is ..." I glance at Max. "Are you sure this is where I'm supposed to be staying?"

Max points at the boxes piled near the closet—my boxes. "I'm sure." He crosses his arms and props his shoulder against the doorjamb. "Please don't let what happened with my brothers affect you too much. I promise my family isn't a bunch of douchebags. We're all pretty nice. Foster and Easton are just ..." He wavers, tilting his head from side to side.

"Assholes," I offer.

He laughs softly. "I was going to go with spoiled brats, but assholes works, too." He nibbles on his lip, his eyes scanning up and down my body.

If I didn't know any better, I'd wonder if he was checking me out. But I do know better. I know there's no way this gorgeous guy could be checking me out.

"Do you want me to show you where the kitchen is?" he asks. "You've got to be starving."

I nod. "Yeah, actually. That'd be great."

His lips turn upward, then he nods as he retreats back into the hallway.

Foster and Easton are no longer lurking around, something I'm grateful for.

"I really am sorry for what my brothers did to you," Max says as we walk down the hallway. "Give them some time, though, and I'm sure they'll warm up to you."

"It's fine if they don't," I say. When he gives me a perplexed look, I add, "It's not like I'm going to be here for very long. I turn eighteen in six months."

His brows furrow. "And then what?"

I lift a shoulder. "And then I move out."

He combs strands of his hair out of his eyes with his fingers. "But, where will you go?"

I shrug again. "College maybe. I might do a road trip with my friends." I scratch my arm. "I actually really need to get a job so I can save up some cash. This town looks really small, though."

"It is really small. And the people here are really wary about hiring newbies," he says. *There's that word again* ... "If you want a job, you're probably going to have to look in Star Grove."

"How far is that?"

"About forty minutes from here."

I let out a weighted sigh. "Is there a bus that goes there?"

He chuckles, shaking his head. "Nope. The only form of transportation here is by your own car. Or, in my case, a motorcycle."

"Oh." I crinkle my nose.

"If you need a ride somewhere, I'm sure one of us can give you one." He slows to a stop in front of a shut door and lifts his hand to knock. "Or you can just borrow one of my dad's many, many cars."

Yeah right. I'm nowhere near comfortable asking to borrow a vehicle. I'm just going to have to figure out another way or beg for someone to hire me here.

"He won't mind," Max insists, knocking on the door. "My dad's a nice guy."

"Yeah, he seems like it," I agree, but that still doesn't mean I'm going to ask to borrow his car.

Smiling, he leans closer to the door. "Hey, Mom, I got Skylin out of her room. I'm going to take her down to the kitchen to get her something to eat."

"Oh, thank goodness," Emaline says breathlessly. I hear a couple of loud crashes, and then the door is cracked open and she peers out.

Her hair is a wild mess, her cheeks are flushed, and her breaths are coming out in a rush.

My mom once opened her bedroom door like that and looked the same way. I think it was because her and my dad were having sex.

My discomfort goes from a ten to an eleven hundred.

An ounce of relief washes over her face as she sees me. "Skylin, honey, I am so sorry for whatever happened. Rest assured, though, all my children are going to be extremely nice to you from now on."

I nod, even though I highly doubt that's going to be the case. But I'm not about to protest because, for one, I'm a guest in this house; and two, I'm pretty certain she was just in the middle of having sex with Gabe and I want this conversation to end as quickly as possible.

She smiles at me, but when her gaze glides to Max, her lips sink. "Can you do me a favor? After you show Skylin where the kitchen is, can you run out to the garage and get me that box we picked up the other day."

Max tenses. "You need that right now?"

Emaline nods, pressing him with a look of urgency. "It's kind of an emergency."

Max bobs his head up and down, worry masking his features. "Yeah, give me a second."

"Just try to hurry—" Emaline winces. "Please."

With a brisk nod, Max spins on his heels and high-tails it down the hallway.

As Emaline shuts the door, I rush after him.

"Is everything okay?" I ask, practically jogging to keep up with his long strides.

He nods as he trots down the stairs. "Yeah, I just need to hurry and get that box up to my mom before she … has a fit."

Emaline doesn't really seem like the type to have a fit over something so trivial, but I've only known her for a day and I barely know Max, so I opt to keep my thoughts to myself.

Max seems content with my silence as he rushes through the house, hurrying across the foyer and through a door located at the back of the house. He motions me inside then flips on a light, revealing a spacious kitchen with marble countertops and stainless-steel appliances.

"Just wait right here," he says in a rush. "I'll get my mom's box then have Charlotte come in and make you something to eat."

"I can fix something myself …" My words fade as he dashes out of the room.

Wrapping my arms around myself, I make my way across the kitchen, heading for the fridge. I feel weird just going through their food, but I feel even weirder about the idea of someone cooking something just for me.

When I open the fridge, though, I immediately regret my decision.

"What on earth ...?" My eyes widen at the glass jars covering the shelves, each filled with oddly textured substances, like glittering purple liquid, oozing green cream, and ... Wait. Is that a jar of ...? "Eyeballs? Oh, my God." I slap my hand over my mouth as I slam the fridge shut, breathing profusely and fighting back the urge to vomit.

Once I get myself calmed the hell down, I dig my phone out of my pocket and send Nina and Gage a group text.

Me: So, is there any reason in particular why someone would keep a jar of eyeballs in their fridge?

Nina: Oh, my God, please don't tell me your new parentals have eyeballs in their fridge!

Me: I could tell you that, but I'd be lying.

Nina: Gah! So gross! What a bunch of freaks! The bodies those eyeballs belong to are probably buried in the basement or something.

My gaze instinctively drops to the floor as images of what Nina said flood my thoughts. Then the vibration of my phone pulls me back to reality.

Gage: Will you chill out? They probably just have them in there to eat.

Me: And that's better because …?

Gage: Well, it's gross, for sure, but in some cultures, eyeballs are a delicacy. Well, animal eyeballs are anyway. I'm hoping you're not talking about human eyeballs.

Me: I'm not sure. I barely got a look at them before I nearly puked.

Nina: Maybe you better check.

Me: No thanks.

Nina: Sky! You have to look! If they have human eyes in their fridge, then they're probably murderers and you won't have to live with them anymore.

Me: Yeah, probably, because they'll kill me.

Nina: I'm sure they won't …

Yeah, the ellipsis at the end of her message is making me feel super great right now.

Gage: Sky, don't listen to her. I'm sure they're just animal eyeballs. But just for peace of mind, you should look.

Me: How am I even supposed to tell if they're human?

Gage: Animals will probably be rounder.

Me: What are you? An animal eyeball expert?

Gage: I'm an expert of everything. I thought you knew that already. ;)

A small smile forms on my lips but promptly fizzles when I look back at the fridge.

"Gage is probably right. They're just animal eyeballs," I mumble as I wrap my fingers around the handle of the fridge and pull the door open—

"What're you doing?" a low voice asks from behind me.

"Fucking hell." I reel around, startled, and press my hand to my chest.

The instant my eyes find the owner of the voice, my pulse speeds even more, and thunder grumbles from outside. I'm not even positive why my heart rate spikes, other than this guy is shockingly pretty in a way that I thought only existed in fairy tales or some shit like that.

Short, blond hair; full, pierced lips; and lavender eyes a similar shade to Emaline's. He's also tall and lean, and his skin is heavily inked with similar tattoos as Max's.

Good Lord, are all the Everettsons gorgeous? And,

why are all their eye colors so vibrant? It makes all other eyes I've ever seen seem dull.

He cocks his head to the side as his gaze sweeps up my body. Then his lips spread into a grin that I can't tell for sure if it's friendly or malicious.

"You must be Skylin."

I nod, shifting my weight. "Yeah."

His grin magnifies. "I'm Porter."

"Oh." I relax a smidgeon. "You're the oldest, right?"

He musingly smiles for some reason. "Yeah, I guess I am." He studies me for a thunder boom of a second before gracefully rounding the island and coming to a stop in front of me. "So, what exactly were you doing in there?" He nods at the fridge without taking his eyes off me.

"Um ..." I'm finding it really hard to concentrate. "I was just going to make myself something to eat."

"But something scared you, right?"

How the hell did he know?

"I'm guessing it was the eyeballs," he says with a grin.

I bob my head up and down. "I've just never seen eyeballs in a fridge before ... or out of a head ..."

He chuckles. "Most people haven't."

"So ... why do you have a jar full of them in your fridge?"

Wetting his lips with his tongue, he reaches for me —or, at least I think he's reaching for me—but then he places his hand against the shut door of the fridge so his arm's resting right beside my head.

"What would you say if I told you they were in there because I like to occasionally eat them?" he asks amusedly.

Wait ... Did he somehow see the conversation I was having with Nina and Gage? No, there's no way.

"Um, I'd say ... cool?" It comes out more of a question.

He studies me intently with his head tilted to the side, then a chuckle slips from his lips. "Cool, huh? That's the only reaction I get?"

"What do you want me to do?" I wonder, my heart thumping in my chest for some crazy-ass reason.

He bites down on his bottom lip hard. "That, honey, is a very dangerous question." He tucks a strand of my hair behind my ear, his eyes fixed on my mouth as he ...

Wait ... Is he *purring?*

"Porter, what're you doing?" The sound of Max's voice makes the haziness that's clouding my mind dissolve.

I blink, realizing how loudly I'm breathing and how hard my heart is knocking against my chest.

Porter rubs his lips together, his gaze briefly

descending to my lips before he pushes away from me. "I was just introducing myself to our new, adorable houseguest." When he glances at Max, Max quirks an eyebrow. "What?" Porter says innocently, but the grin on his face suggests he's anything but innocent.

I just wish I knew why.

These guys are odd. For reals, I feel like I've just moved in with the *Addams Family* or something.

"Fine, I'll back off," Porter says through a laugh. Then he turns to me and lightly tugs on a strand of my hair. "If you want something to eat besides eyeballs, there's another fridge in the pantry."

I'm still not certain if he's joking about eating the eyeballs, and the confusion on my face only makes his amusement double.

Grinning, he strolls away, lightly nudging his shoulder against Max's as he passes. Max responds with a shake of his head and a small crack of a smile.

Once Porter has exited the kitchen, Max focuses on me. "The fridge behind you? That's where we keep Holden and Hunter's science experiment stuff."

"They need eyeballs for experiments?"

"They're … science majors," he says as if that explains everything.

Maybe it does. I'm not too into science, so I'm not an expert. It seems weird to me, though, to keep eyeballs in the fridge. And what was all that other stuff in there?

"Okay ... Sorry I got into it." I feel the need to apologize.

He relaxes, a smile breaking out across his face. "You don't need to apologize. You're welcome to anything in this house. I'd just recommend staying out of that fridge. The stuff Hunter and Holden store in there can be sort of ..."

"Vomit-inducing?" I suggest.

He chuckles. "Yeah, probably to most people." He assesses me briefly before signaling for me to follow him as he enters an alcove. "This is where we keep the more edible stuff." He points at a fridge tucked into the corner. "You can get whatever you want out of it, but Charlotte will be more than happy to make you something whenever." He slants against the fridge and crosses his arms. "She's an excellent cook."

"Thanks for the offer," I say, "but I'm not really used to people cooking for me. In fact, I've been cooking for myself since I was about five or six."

His expression plummets. "Please tell me it was all microwaveable stuff."

I shake my head. "But it's not that big of a deal. My parents taught me how to use the stove before they started letting me cook with it." The frown remains on my face, and my defenses go up. "My parents were—

are good people," I state defensively. "They just like to go out a lot, so I needed to learn how to cook for myself or I'd have ended up living off PB&J sandwiches, which are yummy and everything, but not really a good source for dinner."

His lips tug into an artificial smile. "Well, if you want to cook for yourself, that's fine. But promise me you'll at least let Charlotte cook for you one time, preferably dinner." He smiles for real this time. "She makes some killer pesto pasta and potatoes."

"All right," I say. "That sounds doable, I guess."

He's all amusement again as he moves away from the fridge and opens the door. "There are some leftovers in here from dinner if you want me to heat them up. It's spaghetti and meatballs and some garlic bread." He pulls out a couple of Tupperware containers.

"I can heat them up." I take them from him.

He sighs, shaking his head. "You're stubborn, aren't you?"

I crinkle my nose. "Am I? I mean, I know my friend Nina always says I am, but she's stubborn, too, so I can never trust her opinion."

"You are a little bit." He nudges me back into the kitchen then walks over and opens a cupboard above the sink and takes out a plate. "It's probably a good thing. Us Everettsons are known for our stubbornness, and if you were too much of a pushover, we'd probably end up walking all over you." He sets the plate down then takes the containers with the spaghetti from me, popping open the lid. "You should probably push back the most with Foster and Easton. They're the most likely to stomp all over you if you let them. Like with the attic thing. When they told you that was your room, you should've told them to go fuck themselves."

"I may have if they were one of my friends or maybe even my mom or dad, but ..." I dither, chewing on my bottom lip. "I'm not as stubborn and pushy with people I don't know very well."

"Are you saying you're shy?"

"I don't know ... A lot of people say I am, but personally, I just think I'm quiet." I pause. "I've always kind of sucked at socializing."

"Any particular reason why?"

"What do you mean?"

He opens a drawer and collects a spoon. "Sometimes when people have trouble socializing, it's because of a bad, perhaps even traumatic, experience." He shovels a spoonful of spaghetti onto the plate.

"Are you a psych major?" I question, opening the lid on the container with the garlic bread.

He chuckles as he piles more spaghetti onto the plate. "Actually, I'm not in college. But I do get that a lot, probably because I'm a know-it-all." He winks at me then picks up a piece of garlic bread, puts it onto the plate, and then places the plate in the microwave.

I realize that, whether intentional or not, he just made dinner for me.

"I could've heated that up myself."

"It was just as easy for me to do it." He closes the microwave then pushes some buttons.

And he says I'm stubborn. Clearly, he's just as bad.

Sighing, I plop down on a barstool. "So, if you're not in college, what do you do?"

From the other side of the island, he rests his arms on top of the counter, his eyes glistening mischievously. "What if I told you absolutely nothing? Would you think less of me?"

"No, but I do think that sounds sort of boring." I cross my arms on top of the counter. "But I'm guessing you're lying to me."

His eyes twinkle again. "And why's that?"

"Because of that little twinkle in your eye." I point at his face.

He struggles not to grin. "What twinkle?"

I roll my eyes. "Like you don't already know."

"Maybe I don't," he teases. "Perhaps you're the first person to ever point that out to me."

"I highly doubt that." The lightness in my voice is a bit unfamiliar, but talking to Max is surprisingly easy. "I have a feeling you have that twinkle in your eyes a lot."

"And I have a feeling you're going to be a very amusing addition to this household." He pushes back from the counter as the microwave beeps. "For the record, though, you're right. I don't just sit around and do nothing." He removes the plate from the microwave and sets it down in front of me, along with a fork. "I have a job."

I twirl the noodles around my fork. "What do you do?"

"Hmm ..." He leans back against the counter behind him and rubs his jawline. "I think I won't tell you yet."

"Why?" A teasing grin touches my lips. "Are you, like, a secret agent or something?" I'm only kidding, but when he doesn't answer right away, I have to wonder. "Wait. Are you?"

He shakes his head, strands of his hair falling into his eyes. "Nah, I'm way too rebellious to work for the police. Not to mention, I'd get bored."

I'm about to point out that a secret agent doesn't seem like a boring job when a loud shriek echoes across the house. Max's body immediately stiffens.

"Stay right here, okay?" he says as he hurries toward the door.

"Why? What was that?" I hiss, clutching my fork.

"Just stay here." He rushes out of the room, the door swinging shut behind him.

As another shriek ripples through the air, I retrieve my phone from my pocket and tap open the group message.

Me: Okay, shit's getting crazy here. Now I hear screaming! And Max, one of the guys who lives here, just told me to stay in the kitchen, then ran out in the direction of the screaming.

Gage: Holy shit, dude. Maybe you should, I don't know, like leave or something.

Nina: Or call the effing police! What the hell? First eyeballs in the fridge and then screaming?

Me: I also overheard them whispering about how they're worried I'll find out their secrets. This family is weird. I mean, the mom and dad seem nice, and Max is okay, but Porter seemed weird, and Foster and Easton are asshats. They made me think the attic was my room!

Nina: Jerks. I knew they were gonna be like that, though. They're totally Greys.

Me: Yeah, I think so, too. Man, guys,

this sucks. I already miss home, and it hasn't even been twenty-four hours yet.

Nina: We miss you, too, and we're really worried.

Gage: Has the screaming stopped yet? Do you know what it was?

I glance up, realizing the house is silent now. Eerily silent, as if no one lives here.

Me: Yeah, it stopped. I'm still not even sure what it was, though.

Gage: Makes me really wonder what kind of eyeballs those are in the fridge.

Nina: Gage, why would you say that! She's already freaking out!

Me: I'm not freaking out. I'm just … uneasy. Maybe I'm being paranoid, though.

Nina: No fucking way. If I found eyeballs in the fridge and heard screaming, I'd have bolted by now.

Me: Oh, trust me, I want to.

"Hey." Emaline pops her head into the room, smiles at me, and then walks all the way in.

Me: Gotta go. Someone just walked in. TTYL.

Nina: You better. Seriously, I'm worried.

Gage: Please be careful …

"Are you talking to your friends?" she asks as she makes her way into the kitchen.

I nod, stuffing my phone back into my pocket. "Yeah. I was just telling them I got here safely." A lie, but I'm not about to confess what I was really talking about.

"They must be good friends if they're worried about your safety." She walks up to me and folds her arms. "I just want you to know that, while there's a lot of chaos in this house, you're still safe with us. And if you have any questions at all, please ask. I don't want you to feel uncomfortable." She places her hand on mine. "I've always wanted a daughter, and while I know I can never replace your mom, I'd like us to be friends."

"Okay ... I do have one question." Well, one that I'm daring to ask. "What was that shrieking I heard earlier?"

At first, she appears clueless, but then recognition lights up her eyes, and she chuckles. "That was Easton."

"Is he okay?"

She gives my hand a squeeze. "While my boys love to pull pranks on people, they don't handle it well when they're on the receiving end." A wary look crosses her face. "Do me a favor? Lock your bedroom door tonight, okay? While I'd like to believe my boys won't try to prank you, there's always a tiny chance they'll try."

"Okay." I eye her over, questioning if she's being serious.

She sure looks like she is, and that makes my worry skyrocket.

So, I have to lock the door when I'm sleeping. Yeah, if I wasn't already uneasy about living here, I sure as hell am now.

CHAPTER 11

THAT NIGHT, AFTER I CHANGE INTO MY PAJAMAS, I slip into bed with the door locked. My belly is full of yummy spaghetti and garlic bread, and the mattress is more comfortable than any I've ever slept on. Maybe that's why the sky is so content, just stars and moonlight twinkling against the darkness.

Even though I had a pretty long nap today, my eyelids feel extremely heavy. I'm so close to dozing off when I hear voices just outside my window.

Confused, I climb out of bed, pad over to the window nook, and peer outside. The view from my bedroom is directly into the backyard, which is acres and acres of land that stretches toward a thick forest. And hurrying across the land toward the trees are three figures, one significantly taller than the other two, although all appear on the taller side. And all are wearing hoods pulled over their heads, as if they're trying to keep their identities concealed.

I start to back away, worried they're thieves or something, when one of the figures comes to a stop and turns to look at me.

Bright, glowing, green eyes collide with mine.

Max?

Sleep ...

That's the last thing I remember before darkness overcomes me.

HAVE YOU EVER WOKEN UP FEELING AS THOUGH you have a hangover, yet you never drank the night before? Well, that's about how I feel the next morning when my eyes blink open.

It takes me a second to get my bearings, to remember that I moved in with the Everettsons. Then, a second later, my head begins to throb.

"God, I feel like shit," I mumble, rolling onto my side and retrieving my phone off the nightstand. When I note the time, I wonder if I somehow did get drunk last night and just don't remember.

"Two thirty in the fucking afternoon? How did I sleep so late?" I rub my eyes and blink a couple of times, attempting to clear some of the disorientation from my mind.

It takes a couple of minutes before I have a clear enough head to get out of bed. Then I grab a pair of black pants and a grey tank top before heading toward the bathroom to take a shower.

Emaline showed me which bathroom was mine last night. And I mean *mine* in the literal sense. Apparently, there are enough bathrooms in this house to go around, so I get my very own. I've never had my own bathroom, so it's a bit weird, but I'm pretty grateful I don't have to share with any of the Everettson brothers.

After I shower, get dressed, and comb my hair, I make my way downstairs to get some breakfast. By the time I make it to the main floor, I begin to wonder if perhaps no one is home. When I push into the kitchen, I realize my assumption is correct.

Taped on the front of the fridge is a note:

Hey Sky!

Just wanted to let you know that we'll be gone for most of the day for a baseball tournament (I think Gabe mentioned it yesterday). Help yourself to whatever you need, and if you'd like Charlotte to make you some lunch, just push the buzzer near the fridge. You can also wander around and get familiar with the house. Just steer clear of the basement because we're having issues with mice. There's a pool out back in the garden room if you'd like to go for a swim.

If you need to get ahold of any of us, there's a list of all our numbers in the note section on the iPad on the counter, along with the passcode to the house alarm in case you need to set it. If you wouldn't mind adding your phone number to the list, that'd be fantastic. That way, we can get ahold of you, too.

We won't be home until late this evening. If you're not awake by then, know that we'll be leaving for school around seven thirty tomorrow morning. I'll drive you tomorrow so we can talk to the principal and whatnot. After that, you can ride with Easton and Foster, who have assured me that they'll show you the ropes of Farealee Land Academy.

And if you need anything at all, just let me know! That's what I'm here for!

— Emaline

Crap, somewhere between the madness and moving, I completely forgot that I'll be attending a new school. And an academy apparently. Not that I'm even sure what the difference is between one and a public school. Still, it makes me nervous.

"Please say you're here for me," a succulent voice sails over my shoulder, startling me so badly I nearly jolt out of my skin.

Whirling around, I find a tall, lean guy with short

brown hair standing near the door. He's wearing a long-sleeved, grey shirt with the sleeves rolled up, black pants, thick boots, and his intense golden eyes are meticulously skimming over me.

"Um ..." I shift my weight, scratching at my arm.

The edges of his lips kick up into a grin. "You might be the best present I've gotten yet."

I blink. "Huh?"

He grins, his lips parting. "I think I—"

The door behind him swings open and in walks a guy who looks like the other guy's doppelganger. The only visible difference I can see is their outfits; the guy who entered sporting a navy blue, long-sleeved shirt instead of a grey one, and he has on jeans and Converse sneakers.

So, these are the identical twins.

"Hey, Hunter, what do you think about ...?" He trails off as his gaze finds mine. "What is this?" he asks, deliberately scanning me over in confusion.

"I think Max got us an early birthday present," the other guy—Hunter—sucks his lip between his teeth. "He did good this year. Way better than last year."

Holden's brows dip and I notice the scar Gabe was talking about. "Are you sure that's what she is? She's unreadable."

Hunter tips his head to the side as he assesses me. "Yeah, I didn't notice that before, but she is, isn't she?"

Holden nods then asks me, "What are you?"

Puzzlement webs through my mind. *What am I? Doesn't he mean who?*

I cross my arms over my chest. "I'm Skylin."

Holden's lips form an *O*.

"My, my, when Mom and Dad told us they'd be taking in someone as a favor to an old friend, I didn't expect this," Hunter says with a grin.

"Careful, Hunt." A warning seeps into Holden's tone as he throws a sharp look at his brother. After staring down a grinning Hunter for the most awkwardly silent minute ever, Holden sighs then focuses on me. "Hey." He steps toward me with his hand outstretched. "I'm Holden, and this"—he nods at the other guy—"is Hunter. I'm sorry for being weird. We were just a little bit confused ... We thought you weren't going to be here until tomorrow."

I guess that sort of explains their confusion, but I still don't understand what they meant when they said I was unreadable. And Max said something similar to me last night.

"It's nice to meet you." I shake his hand, getting distracted by the sparkly warmth flowing up my arm.

Through the skylight above, the sunlight suddenly seems brighter.

What the hell?

Holden casts a glance upward, his brows knitting,

but then he returns his gaze to me and a smile graces his lips. "I know the circumstance of you having to stay with us isn't great, but I just want you to know that we're glad to have you here."

Thank God. He's actually nice.

"Thanks."

A bit of relief douses over me until Hunter steps forward, snatches my hand from Holden, and kisses my knuckles.

"Tu mi, sint satis est splendidis stellis."

"Oh, for the love of gods," Holden groans. "Sky, just ignore him."

"Since I have no fucking clue what he said, that's pretty doable," I say, eliciting a chuckle from them both.

"She's cute," Hunter says to Holden. "Can I keep her?"

Cute? No guy has ever called me cute. Well, except for Gage, but he doesn't count.

My cheeks flood with heat.

Shit. Am I blushing?

Hunter grins. "Yeah, I'm definitely keeping her."

Holden heaves a sigh. "Hunt, you can't keep her." He looks at me. "Sorry, he doesn't come with a filter. You get used to it, though. Or, well, you learn to just ignore it."

I nod, my skin growing hotter as Hunter's gaze continues to devour me.

A phone buzzes from somewhere, but Hunter's eyes never waver from me, even when he sticks his hand into his pocket and pulls out his phone. Holden does the same thing, and I let a gradual breath ease past my lips as they both focus on their phones.

"Shit, we're late," Holden mutters then stuffs his phone back into his pocket. "We need to get out there."

"Nah, I think I might skip this ... tournament," Hunter replies, giving me a strange look that I can't quite decipher. "I'll stay here and keep Skylin company."

"No, you won't." Holden elbows his brother in the side, causing Hunter to blast him with a dirty look. "You need to be part of this *tournament*. You're way out of practice."

Hunter rolls his eyes but backs toward the door. "Sky, it was a pleasure meeting you. We'll have to do something together soon. Something fun that'll make you blush again." He winks at me then pushes through the doors.

Holden blows out an exhausted exhale then shakes his head. "It really was nice meeting you, and I hate to take off like this when we haven't even properly met, but this tournament is really important."

"I totally understand," I say, waving him off.

He wavers, chewing on his bottom lip. "Maybe I could show you around town tomorrow night and show you where all the good places to eat are and the places to avoid."

"I'd like that." And I mean it. Holden seems nice, and I'd really like to look around town and see if anyone's hiring.

"Awesome." He smiles then pushes out the door.

The sparkly warmth that was flowing up my arm instantly fizzles, leaving me to wonder what caused it to begin with.

Maybe it's a new, little trait to my abilities?

Frowning at the idea that my abilities could be growing, I turn toward the fridge to get something to eat, but pause when I glance out the window and spot Hunter and Holden hiking across the field out back.

I squint against the sunlight as I lean toward the window. Is the tournament out there somewhere? That'd be kind of weird, though, since there isn't much out there except a forest.

My suspicions only grow when Holden and Hunter reach the border of the trees. As they're about to slip into forest, they glance back at the house the lift their hands in front of them. The air ripples like water, making the trees sway and the sunlight flicker. Then they lower their hands and step forward into the trees.

My jaw just about smacks the floor.

What the heck did I just see? Because it almost looked like they walked through ... well, like a portal or something.

Backing away from the window, I massage my temples.

I'm losing my damn mind. What I saw couldn't be real.

But as panic sets in and the sky abruptly shadows with clouds, I'm reminded of the strange occurrences that I see every day. Maybe other strange things exist out there, too. Maybe the Everettsons are strange.

They sure as hell seem like it.

Sucking in a breath, I leave the kitchen. Later, looking back to that moment, I'll wonder what on earth compelled me to do it. Maybe it was the simple fact that I was tired and emotionally drained. Or maybe it was something more than that. A feeling. A whisper begging me to go see.

See that I wasn't as alone as I thought I was.

CHAPTER 12

T HE WIND PICKS UP AS I STRIDE ACROSS THE
grassy field, the chilled air nipping at my skin. I probably should've put on a jacket, but if I turn back now, I'll more than likely talk myself out of doing this. So, wrapping my arms around myself, I hurry toward the forest where the trees sway with the wind.

When I reach the border, I pause, just like Hunter and Holden did, and move to elevate my hand.

Part of me questions if I hallucinated the rippling effect, that when I place my palm in the air, nothing will happen. But just like with Holden and Hunter, the air ripples like waves. It also feels warm against my skin, as if begging me to touch it longer.

My insides jitter with nerves, and the sky more than notices, lighting up like the Fourth of July.

Calm down, Sky, or you're going to start a fire.

Summoning a deep breath, I step forward and through the rippling, clear wall.

Swoosh.

The second my foot enters the trees, sparkling warmth waterfalls over me. I'd be more concerned about it, except the scene in front of me has me very distracted.

The trees are taller than I've ever seen, the grass is greener than the greenest of shades, and the number of colorful flowers sprouting from everywhere is unnatural.

When I look up, my lips part in shock. The sky is an electric blue, not a single cloud evident.

"What is this place?" I whisper, peering around.

A few butterflies flutter around a rose bush, but other than that, I can't see any signs of life. Water is flowing from somewhere close by, and when I listen closer, I hear faint voices drifting through the gentle breeze. I can't make out what they're saying or who they belong to so, putting my guard up, I endeavor deeper into the trees.

With each step, the colors of the forest sharpen, as if I've stepped into a portrait. And the voices also get louder, the faint murmurs turning into actual words.

"Just get in the middle, okay?" Gabe sounds as if he's losing his patience.

A flutter of a second later, I slam to a halt as I reach the edge of a small clearing where all the Everettsons are standing in a circle. They're dressed head to toe in black with hoods pulled over their heads, which I find odd for several different reasons, one being that Hunter and Holden weren't wearing hoodies when they left the house.

Before they can spot me, I hunker down behind a tree and trap my breath in my chest. I'm not even sure why my instinct is to hide, or what I'm afraid of, other than this entire situation is straight-up crazy.

Maybe I'm crazy.

Maybe I'm hallucinating.

Maybe I'm still asleep in my bed, dreaming.

I pinch my arm to check and wince. *Fuck, that hurt.*

"I don't know why we have to do this," Foster growls out. "I've been getting better."

"We know, son, but with all the storms that have been blowing through ..." Gabe gives a short pause. "I think it's best if we practice containing your powers, okay?"

"I already said I'm not causing those storms," Foster bites out. "Something else is doing it."

Silence momentarily stills the air.

"Sweetie, as far as everyone knows, you're the only elemental enchanter alive right now," Emaline says.

"So, if the storms are being controlled, it's probably your doing. Not that we're mad at you—we know you've been stressed out lately. But we need to get your powers under control before you draw too much attention, which can't happen. And while we'll do anything to protect our secrets, I'd rather just make sure they stay secret."

"Fine. Whatever," Foster grumbles. "Let's just get this over with."

A quietness settles across the land.

Wondering what they could possibly be doing, I muster up every ounce of courage I possess and peer around the tree trunk I'm hiding behind.

Nothing could prepare me for what I see.

Foster has moved into the center of the circle, and his hands are crackling with lightning bolts. That's not even the strangest part. Each Everettson has their hands out in front of them, and a ray of light is streaming from their palms and toward Foster. Even crazier? The rays of light match their eye colors.

"Holy shit," I gasp out as I slowly back away.

Blue and silver electricity cracks across the sky, and I tense, trying to get my breathing under control.

Calm down. You're going to be just fine.

Foster's eyes snap open, and his lightning charged gaze welds with mine. He looks possessed. Demonic.

I recall the screams I heard last night.

Just who the hell are the Everettsons?

Panicking, I reel around and run like hell in the direction I came from, not looking back, even when I hear cursing from behind me.

When I stumble from the trees, I rush back toward the house and barrel inside. Then I sprint straight up to my room and start shoving my clothes into a backpack.

I need to get the hell out of here. Now. I can't be here ... not after what I just saw. Not when I have no clue what they were doing. Plus, I'm worried they might hurt me for finding out their secret. After all, I heard Max, Easton, and Foster verbalizing their concern for me discovering their family's secrets. This has to be to what they were referring. I mean, what else could it be?

The idea that there could very well be even more to this makes me shiver.

Grabbing my phone, I send Nina and Gage a text.

Me: Can someone pick me up? It's an emergency.

I move to hit send when my phone powers down. And not because it has a dead battery.

"Fuck. I need to get out of here." My heart thumps in my chest as I shove my phone into my pocket, sling my bag over my shoulder, and hightail it out of the house.

My plan is to run to town and borrow someone's phone so I can call Nina and Gage and tell them to come get me. Where I'll go from there, I haven't got a clue. But I'll figure it out.

But what if they come looking for me? What if they find me? What will they do to me?

I swallow hard at the many ideas flowing through my mind and accelerate from a run to a full-on sprint.

By the time I reach the gated entrance, which is thankfully open, a hailstorm is blowing in. With how upset I am, I'm not shocked. In fact, I wouldn't be surprised if a blizzard soon blew in.

Positioning my bag over my head, I squeeze through the gates and run out onto the street. Chips of ice plink against my body, pelting my arms and legs, but I continue on, my breaths fogging out in front of my face as the temperature plummets.

I don't make it very far before Gabe's truck pulls up behind me, the windshield wipers moving a million miles a minute against the hail.

I quicken my pace, refusing to slow down, and deliberate whether or not to duck into the trees lining the road to escape them.

"Sky!" Gabe calls out over the hammering hail.

Doors slam shut, and then footsteps thud against the asphalt behind me.

I run faster, the sizes of the hail growing bigger.

"Sky, wait up!" Max shouts. "Fuck, what is with this hail?"

"You don't need to be afraid of us," Holden yells after me. "Please, just slow down so we can talk."

Jesus, are they all here?

Daring a glance behind me, I see Gabe, Max, and Holden. That makes me feel a drop better, since the three of them have been fairly nice to me.

"Sweetheart, just relax, okay?" Max jogs after me, the hood of his jacket pulled over his head. Hail is plinking off him, yet he appears unbothered—they all do. "We know what you saw looks really ..." He wavers. "Odd."

"And it is odd," Holden clarifies, jogging beside Max. He's pulled his hood down; little drops of ice cover his hair. "But we promise we won't hurt you."

As a hail pegs me straight between the eyes, I slow to a stop. "Mother effer, that hurt."

"Are you okay?" Holden asks worriedly as he jogs up to me.

I hold up my hand and skitter back. "Just stay away from me."

They all slow to a stop and cautiously raise their hands in front of them.

"Sky, if you'll come back to the house with us," Gabe says, walking toward us, "we'll explain what you just saw."

Max's and Holden's heads whip in his direction, surprise flickering across their expressions.

They weren't expecting him to say that.

"Dad ..." Max starts with reluctance, his eyelashes fluttering as hail pegs him in the face.

Gabe holds his hand up in Max's direction. "Your mother and I already talked about this and decided that we can't keep this from her. Not when she's going to be living with us for months." He lowers his hand to his side. "We should've just told her to begin with, but we were waiting for the right time ..." He presses his lips together and shakes his head. "I'm sorry you had to find out that way, Sky. I'm sure what you saw was ... frightening."

Actually, what I saw wasn't necessarily frightening. It was the worry of what they'd do to me if they found out I saw that sent me running.

"Dad, humans can't understand." Max presses, crossing his arms. "You of all people should know that."

Humans? So, they aren't human? I guess, when I really think about it, I'm not that surprised.

"Actually, they can." Gabe looks at me while wiping melted hail from his face. "Skylin's father and mother knew about us."

My jaw drops. "They did?"

He nods, inching toward me, ice crunching underneath his boots. "I was once captured by some hunters who wanted to do experiments on me. Their experiments almost killed me, and probably would've, if your father hadn't rescued me."

Hearing his story makes me relax enough that the hail shifts to rain.

My dad and mom knew about this? He saved Gabe and kept Gabe's secret? That means they won't hurt me ... I hope.

I lower my bag from my head, and raindrops dot my skin. "And, what are you exactly?"

Gabe glances at Holden and Max, who are bursting with tension, then redirects his attention back to me. "We're elemental protectors. Max is wind, Porter and my wife are ice, Easton and I are water, Holden and Hunter are fire, and Foster is ... well, he's complicated, but I'll explain that later."

"You're the only elemental enchanter alive right now," Emaline had said to Foster in the forest.

They had also blamed the storms on him. Could it be that Foster controls storms? Could I be like Foster? Do the Everettsons know about my ability? Doubtful since, not only did they just refer to me as human, but they think Foster is responsible for all the storms.

"Foster really needs to practice controlling his abilities more," Max utters as he peers up at the cloudy sky.

Yeah, they definitely don't know about me. I could tell them, but something holds me back. I'm not even sure what. Years of silence? The fear of knowing the truth about myself? The fear of finding out I'm not like them and am a freak of nature?

One thing is certain; I have a choice to make right now. I can run away from them and the truth, or trust Gabe and find out what exactly it is that I saw in the forest.

Part of me wants to keep on running, but deep down, I know that isn't what I'm going to do. I need to trust Gabe and go back with him. After all, if my dad knew about his powers, then he can't be too horrible. Plus, maybe I can find out more about my ability. That is, if I'm like the Everettsons.

"All right, I'll go back with you." I sling the handle of my bag over my shoulder and walk toward them.

Fog laces from their lips as they exhale in relief then turn back for the truck. Me? I'm a nervous fucking wreck as I climb into the truck with them.

All these years, I believed I was the only one with strange powers. Now, come to find out, I'm not. It's a lot to take in. All of this is.

We remain silent for the short ride home. Max and Holden keep throwing worried glances at me, as if expecting me to dive out of the truck or something.

Their attention makes me feel squirmy inside, for several different reasons.

By the time we pull up into the driveway, I'm a jumble of nerves.

When Gabe parks the truck, everyone hops out and hikes up the pathway toward the front door, boots splashing in puddles.

Holden slows down when he nears the steps and waits for me to catch up.

"Are you okay?" he whispers lowly.

Max pauses by the front door and glances over his shoulder at me, waiting for my answer, I'm assuming.

I shrug as the image of them in the forest with their hands lit up flashes through my mind. "I'm really not sure."

Holden squeezes my hand. "Everything's going to be okay, Sky." Despite his words, the hesitancy in his expression has me questioning if he believes his own words. But I don't get too much time to stress about it as he folds his hand around mine and glittery warmth kisses my fingertips.

I bite down on my tongue to keep a gasp from fumbling past my lips.

I don't ... What is that?

Holden doesn't seem to notice my reaction, holding my hand as he steers me past Max.

Gabe pushes the doors open then ushers us

through the foyer and into the massive living room where the rest of the Everettsons are waiting. A fire is crackling in the fireplace, and the air smells of hot chocolate and cinnamon. The scene would feel homey, except for the nervousness trickling through the air.

"Go ahead and have a seat," Gabe tells me while shucking off his jacket.

Swallowing nervously, I peer inside the room.

Easton and Foster are sitting on a sectional sofa, along with Emaline, and Hunter is lounging in a chair, his boots kicked off and his feet kicked up on an ottoman. Mugs are on the coffee table, along with a plate of cookies. And all their gazes are fixed on me. Well, not me per se, but mine and Holden's interlocked fingers.

Shit, I forgot we were holding hands. Probably because the warmth of his touch makes me feel so relaxed.

I wiggle my hand from his grip and stuff my hands into the pockets of my jacket to hide how bad I'm trembling.

"Oh, sweetie." Emaline rises to her feet, whisks across the room, and wraps her arms around me. "I'm so sorry you had to find out this way. We should've told you the moment you came to our home." She hugs me tightly. "I just hope we didn't scare you too badly."

"It's fine." A partial lie, but what else am I supposed to say? "I just ..." I sigh as she pulls back and looks me directly in the eye. "I just don't understand why my parents never mentioned stuff like ... well, whatever you were doing in those trees." If they had said something, maybe I would've told them about my ability a long time ago. Not that we spent a lot of time talking to each other, but we did speak about important stuff sometimes. Now I can't even tell them anything at all.

"They probably didn't mention it because we asked them not to." She smooths my hair out of my eyes. "It's very important that no one finds out about us. If the wrong people did, we could end up experiments in some lab."

"Like Gabe was?" I slip my hands out of my pockets.

Her wide eyes land on Gabe. "You told her that part already?"

He ruffles his damp hair into place. "I thought, if she knew what her father did for me, it'd help her feel a bit better about this."

Emaline nods, her gaze traveling back to me. "So, you understand what's at stake if anyone finds out about us?"

I nod, even though I don't know all the details about what happened to Gabe or who these scientists are. But I've felt that fear myself of someone finding out about me, so I understand where they're coming from.

"I won't tell anyone. I promise." It's the truth. I have no plans of telling anyone about what I saw in the woods. If I did, people would think I was insane.

She smiles. "Thank you. You don't know how much we appreciate this."

Foster glares at me. "Yeah, *if* she keeps her word." His eyes have returned to their normal shade of sky blue, but his gaze is still piercing.

"Foster," Gabe warns in a cold tone. "I trust that Skylin will keep her word, and you will, too."

"Why should we trust her?" Easton asks his dad. "We don't even know her."

"But your mother and I knew her parents, and they've kept our secret for decades." Gabe hangs up his jacket on a nearby coatrack, walks into the room, and then sinks into a chair with his shoulders slumped. "Scott, Skylin's father, was the man who rescued me from the hunters." He rubs his hand across his head. "He saved my life and was—is the most trustworthy person I know. Her mother is equally as trustworthy, and I have no doubt that their daughter is the same way."

The room grows so quiet I can hear the embers in the fire hissing.

"I trust her," Holden utters from beside me.

"Me, too," Max says with his eyes trained on me.

"I really don't know her." Porter shrugs. "However, she let the whole eyeballs-in-the-fridge thing drop pretty easily, even though I could tell she was freaked out by it."

"And the screaming last night," Max adds. "She didn't question that too much."

Yeah, speaking of which, I really want to find out what that was because I'm starting to question if it was because Easton was pranked.

"Maybe she's insane then." Easton smirks at me as he reclines back in the chair with his hands tucked behind his head.

I've seriously had enough of his crap, and with the day I've had …

Anger bursts through like a zap of lightning.

"You know, you've smirked at me so many times that, at this point, I'm actually starting to wonder if it's just how your face looks. Perhaps you did it so many times that your lips just got stuck in that stupid position. Well, either that or you secretly want to look like the Cheshire Cat. Which, if you do, good job. You're almost there." I bite down on my tongue to stop myself from saying anything else.

Easton's brows lift to his hairline in surprise while Max chokes on a laugh, and Emaline grins.

"Good job." She smiles at me, leaving confusion twirling in my mind.

She's glad I basically told Easton to fuck off?

"He'll be easier to deal with now that you've pushed back," Max whispers, leaning toward me.

"You know what, maybe you're not half bad," Easton confirms Max's words.

Foster gives Easton the hardest look ever, but Easton ignores it, grinning at me.

"Why don't you come sit down?" Emaline takes a seat on the sofa again. "I'm sure you have questions."

I make my way into the room and sit down on an empty sofa, feeling as though I'm going to need as much breathing room as possible. But Max and Holden take a seat on either side of me, so there goes that plan. They sit really close to me, too. So close I can feel heat emitting from their bodies, seeping through the fabric of my wet clothes.

Instead of saying something, everyone remains silent, as if waiting for me to speak first.

I pick at my fingernails, trying to figure out what to say next. "Gabe said you're elemental protectors and that you are wind, fire, water, and ice ... But I'm not really sure what that means. Well, not completely anyway."

They all look to Gabe to answer.

He scrubs his hand across his jawline. "Well, to

put it simply, it basically means we're able to control the elements. So, for instance, I can control water and channel my powers from it. So, every spell I cast has to be directly related to the water element. Same with fire, ice, and wind."

"Oh ..." Wow, that was so not what I was expecting. Honestly, I thought he was going to say they were witches or something—it's what it looked like. "So, what were those rays of light you were shooting out of your hands and into Foster? Because I sort of noticed the color of them matched your eyes."

"The color is a representation of our power," Gabe explains, sitting back in the chair. "When you run into other elemental protectors, you'll be able to tell their power just by the color of their eyes."

My jaw nearly bitch-slaps the ground. "There're more of you?"

Gabe gives a nod. "There's a lot actually."

This would be a great time to tell them about my ability, but the words won't pass my lips.

Just say it aloud, Sky. Tell them!

But it's as if my lips are being controlled by an unseen force, and my mouth won't even open.

"You're very tense," Max whispers, rubbing my back.

Everyone is staring at us now, and for some stupid reason, I blush.

Easton smirks, his lips parting, but thankfully, Gabe cuts him off with a string of curses as he fishes his phone from his pocket.

A second later, all the Everettsons are taking out their phones.

"The council at headquarters has called an emergency meeting," Gabe mutters as he reads a text. He glances up at Emaline, and they trade a cryptic look. "It says everyone needs to attend."

Worry floods Emaline's face. "I wonder what it could be about."

"I have no idea, but we need to go." Gabe stands and puts his phone away.

Emaline pushes to her feet. "We can't just leave Sky here by herself."

"I'll be fine," I lie. I'm not sure I'll ever be fine again.

I'm not even sure if I was ever fine.

Gabe rakes his fingers through his hair. "Actually, the council is requesting that Sky come, too."

Silent tension electrifies around the room.

"Why?" Holden finally breaks the silence.

"I'm not sure." Gabe casts a worried glance in my direction. "I guess we'll find out, though." He looks at Emaline. "We just need to make sure we're careful while we're there... you know how things are there." When she nods worriedly, I gulp. Then Gabe turns to me. "I know this is going to sound a bit weird but, would you mind putting on something that has a bit of steel in it?"

Like my necklace?

"Why?" I ask warily.

He scratches between his brows. "Where we're going ... your body will be able to handle it better if you have steel on you."

My nervousness slams through the roof, my palms beginning to sweat. "Where are we going? And what is this council?"

They all exchange an uneasy look, and then Emaline says, "We're going to our homeland, which technically isn't in this world. And as for the council... They're basically like our form of government is the best way to put it. Well, they have been for the last couple of decades."

And just like that, I become painfully aware that nothing is what I ever thought it was. It also makes me question why my mom gave me the steel necklace to begin with. Because she knew that people like the Everettsons existed? Or is there more to it?

Hopefully, I can find out some answers soon because I feel like I'm losing my damn mind.

"Okay, I'll be right back." Since I never put my necklace on after I got out of the shower, I go upstairs to do so.

I feel like I'm in a daze as I return back downstairs, my mind crammed with too many questions. But I immediately get distracted when a shriek cuts through the air. It's kind of like the noise I heard last night, but sounds more inhuman.

Maybe it's a bat in the attic?

Seriously, Sky? Like bats can scream. And besides, after what you just learned, you should probably be thinking more creatively.

"Just ignore it," I whisper to myself.

But as I pass by the room Emaline was in last night, it's pretty clear the noise is coming from in there. Beyond curious, I step toward the door. I almost feel bad for snooping, but not enough to back out. Wrapping my fingers around the doorknob, I push the door open. Or well, try to push the door open, but it's locked.

As the shrieking grows rambunctious, I crouch down and peer through the door lock. What I see makes me question if I am insane, if maybe I did a hit of acid somehow without knowing and have lost my mind. Because on the other side of the door is a room covered in trees and flowers, so thick it looks like a forest is growing in there. But that's not even the craziest part. No, the craziest part is the blond haired man... creature with glittery purple skin and pale blue lips screaming at the top of his lungs.

I gasp, slapping my hand over my mouth. *What is this?*

The man/creature pauses, his gaze flicking toward the door. A grin curls at his lips, and then just like that, one of his beady, purple eyes is peering through the lock at me.

"Hey little enchanted one, why don't you let me out of here?" he purrs.

A chill slithers down my spine, and I trip back, shaking my head. "No way."

"Oh come on," he begs hypnotically. "I promise I don't bite."

I shake my head again, and he completely contradicts himself as he snaps his teeth.

Fuck this shit.

I take off sprinting down the stairs, my feet hammering against the steps.

"Are you okay?" Emaline asks as I enter the room, panting.

Only her, Gabe, and Max are in the room. The rest of the Everettsons are MIA, and a circle of rainbow-tinted light is now funneling in the center of the fireplace instead of a fire.

"Um..." I struggle to catch my breath. "Were you aware there's a screaming... man in your room?"

Her expression drops. "That's not a man. That's a... faerie?" She says it more like a question.

My eyes snap wide. "Faerie's exist?"

Max finds my reaction amusing. "They do. And there's a lot more than just faeries wandering around in this world and other worlds too."

"Oh." I have so many questions yet not a damn one seems to want to leave my lips.

"Will explain more when we get back, okay?" Emaline steps toward me. "Right now, we really need to get going." She nods at the rainbow-tinted light swirling in the fireplace.

I'm uncertain what I expected when Emaline said we'd be leaving this world, but I didn't consider it'd be through some sort of portal in the fireplace.

"Go ahead and walk through the portal, Sky." Emaline points at the circle of rainbow light then offers me an encouraging smile. "My boys are waiting for you on the other side, and Gabe, Max, and I will be right behind you."

I stare at the shimmering light moving like a tornado into the unknown. I attempt to will my feet forward, but my boots feel as heavy as bricks of lead.

Max steps up beside me. "You'll be fine. Just hold my hand, okay?" He laces his fingers through mine.

He doesn't give me any time to back out, tugging me into the light. And all I can do is hold my breath and hope I make it out of this alive.

Hope that I can trust the Everettsons.

CHAPTER 13

Portal traveling? Yeah, if you'd asked me a few days ago if I thought stuff like that existed, I'd have gone with a um... are you crazy? Yeah, I may have powers, but I've also spent most of my life believing I was the only one who did. Turns out, I was wrong.

Way, way wrong...

Entering the portal is a lot like stepping into a hot tub. Bubbly warmth immediately engulfs me, and I swear water seeps through my clothes. Yet, when I stumble out of the rainbow light, my jeans and shirt are dry. Apparently, though, my feet have forgotten how to work, and I end up losing my hold of Max's hand as I trip forward. But arms enclose around me and stop me from falling to the ground.

Whoever is touching me, their nearness causes a jolt of electricity to zap through my body.

"Gods, do you have two left feet or something?" Foster grumbles as he wraps his arm around my waist.

Grimacing, I shove him away. Out of all the Everettsons to catch me, why did it have to be him?

"Your klutziness is going to get you hurt here," Foster continues, crossing his lean arms and glaring at me.

"I'm not that klutzy," I argue. "And even if I am, there're six of you to keep me from getting hurt, so I guess I don't have too much to worry about, do I?" I smirk but, deep down, I'm a bit surprised.

I've never been one for smarting off to people I don't know, but I've done it a couple of times since I've been with the Everettsons. Is it the stress of the situation making me do it? Or are the Everettson brothers bringing out a different side of me? A side I'm not sure I hate or like. Maybe a bit of both.

"You really trust us to protect you?" Foster questions with a raise of his brow.

I shrug. "Sure."

He leans in, his eyes darkening. "Then you're stupider than I thought."

"And you're a bigger asshole than I thought," I quip, curling my fingers into fists.

He smirks. "I thought you would've figured that out after you tried to hit on me back in Honeyton."

My face stupidly floods with heat.

Since he hadn't mentioned the incident before, I assumed he either forgot about it or was just going to pretend it never happened. That was probably pretty damn stupid of me.

"I wasn't hitting on you." Not a total lie. I was planning to hit on him that day, but his immediate rejection put an end to it before it even started. "I was just being friendly."

"Liar." His smirk magnifies as he slants closer, the rainbow portal reflecting in his eyes. "I could tell you wanted me. You still do."

"Actually, I don't." That part is true. Do I think Foster is hot? Absolutely. But I'm in no way attracted to a guy who has called me stupid and treats me like shit. "The second you opened your mouth, any attraction went *poof*." I make a *poofing* gesture with my hand right in his face.

His grin remains. "You do realize you just admitted you were attracted to me, right?"

I lower my hand to my side, my blood boiling. "Yeah? So what? I'm sure you've had a lot of girls attracted to you, but I doubt you've ever had any of them like you for your awesome personality. In fact, I bet most girls lost their attraction to you the second you opened your mouth."

I must have struck a nerve because his smile fades.

I should feel good about pissing him off, but I don't. Nina calls my inability to be a straight-up bitch my weakness, but I'm glad I'm capable of feeling bad. Well, most of the time. Right now, I wish I could hang on to my vindictiveness for a bit longer, but unfortunately, that's not my MO.

I'm about to apologize when Easton appears out of nowhere. "You know, when I first met you, I thought you were sweet. Now I'm wondering if you were just hiding your claws."

"I'm not usually this mean. You guys just bring it out of me." I turn away from them, and my jaw drops. "What the hell?" My eyes widen as I take in the scene before me: the trees that are so tall they appear to touch the sky, the giant mushrooms covering the grassland, the kaleidoscopic sky, and the hundreds of light orbs dancing through the air.

We appear to be standing on a podium with a pearl-like texture. On one side of me is the rainbow portal and standing on my other side is Holden, Hunter, Max, Easton, and Foster. Porter, Emaline, and Gabe are nowhere to be seen.

As I start to ask where the missing three are,

Emaline and Gabe leap from the portal and onto the podium.

"Are you okay?" Emaline promptly surveys me over. "Sometimes portal traveling can do ... weird things to your body."

"What sort of weird things?" I ask worriedly.

Emaline gives a wary glance at Gabe, who shrugs.

"We might as well tell her," he says. "Things are only going to get stranger from here on out."

Emaline directs her focus back to me. "Sometimes portal traveling can alter the construction of a human body. Like, for instance, your legs could end up where your arms are and vice versa. You seem fine, though, since you walked through with Max. But if something did get messed up, we can fix it."

"Why would walking through the portal with Max make it so I'm fine?" I wonder. "Because of his power?"

She nods. "The side effects of portal traveling are less severe if a human walks through with an elemental protector. Or any paranormal, I guess."

Hearing her so casually say the word *paranormal* wigs me out, but something else she says distracts me.

"So, only humans get side effects from portal traveling?" I ask.

"Humans get side effects from most things in our world." Foster is the one to answer, his cold gaze burrowing into me. "Which is why they shouldn't be a part of our world."

"Foster," Gabe reprimands. "You need to lose the attitude."

Foster rolls his eyes. "And we need to lose the human. But no one seems to want to listen to me, so why should I listen to you?"

"Foster!" Emaline gasps in horror.

She's acting as if Foster has never acted so rude in his life, but my bet is he's an asshole most of the time, except for when he's around her.

Foster shrugs her off. "What? It's the truth."

"Young man," Gabe warns, scowling at him. "You will lose the attitude right now and apologize to Sky, or else you'll be grounded for the next two weeks."

"Go ahead and ground me. I'm not going to apologize for something I'm not sorry for." Tossing one final icy look at me, he hops off the podium and drops into the grass. Then he hikes off across the field where the shimmering light orbs are dancing.

"I'll go check on him," Easton says then leaps down into the grass.

"I'm so sorry about that," Emaline apologizes to me. "He's not usually like this."

I catch Hunter and Max rolling their eyes, so I'm betting my early assumption of Foster is correct.

Emaline doesn't notice her sons' eye rolls, though,

as she turns away from me to Gabe. "Do you want to take the long way or the short way?"

Gabe's gaze flicks to me then back to her. "With how busy the city is and how unfriendly everyone is getting toward humans, we better go the long way, just to be safe."

"Am I safe here?" I question nervously, glancing upward as a bolt of lightning blazes across the glittery-blue sky.

"As long as you stay with us, you are," Emaline assures me, but a drop of hesitancy rings in her tone. Then her attention drifts upward. "Is Foster really this upset?"

Again, my lips part to tell them about my powers, to explain that I'm fairly positive Foster isn't causing the lightning storm. But, like before, no words pass my lips.

What is wrong with me? Why can't I just say the damn words aloud?

"I'm not sure Foster's doing it," Hunter mutters, silvery-blue flashes of lightning reflecting in his eyes.

Max glances at him with his head cocked. "Why would you say that?"

Holden lowers his gaze from the sky. "I'm not posi-tive, but it feels like there might be another energy nearby."

They all stiffen, darting their gazes to the trees,

their hands crackling with the same light that I saw earlier when I snuck into the woods. Only, up close, I can see it's not just light radiating from their hands. Holden's and Hunter's palms are actually on fire, golden flames emitting from their flesh. Emaline has flakes of ice twirling in the center of her palms that mixes with the light, and Gabe has droplets of water dewing on his skin, while a small, funneling tornado is twirling around Max's arms.

As the air crackles with heat and the wind howls, the atmosphere grows humid yet somehow chills. I anxiously step away from them, getting sensory overload.

The movement catches Gabe's attention. Frowning, he curls his fingers inward and the light and water dissipate. "Easy, everyone. I think we're making Sky nervous."

"You're fine." But I'm far from fine. Seeing them on edge is making me aware that danger is likely lurking out in … well, wherever the hell we are.

"How could another energy cause lightning?" Max asks, turning his back toward the trees, the light and wind around him dimming as he looks questioningly at Holden. "Only an elemental enchanter can do that."

So, elemental enchanters are the only ones who can create lightning?

I gulp at the realization.

"You guys said that Foster is the only elemental enchanter, right?" If my mouth would've allowed me to, I may have asked if I could be one.

They grow extremely uneasy, shifting their weight and scratching their arms and brows.

"Yeah, he is," Max finally answers, stuffing his hands in his pockets.

Great, if I am like Foster, then that means we're the only two of our kind. I don't want that at all. I don't want to be stuck in a rare category with a guy who's a fucking jerk.

Max glances at Emaline, who chews on her bottom lip worriedly.

"Elemental enchanters have every elemental power inside their veins, which means they're very powerful." She takes both my hands in hers, nervousness emitting from her. "And in our world, the more powerful you are, the more in danger you are of either someone trying to manipulate your powers or being eliminated because of them. It's why no one can know about Foster's powers. The only elemental protectors who do know about him are us and a few others we trust. Well, and Kash." She must note the puzzlement on my face because she adds, "He's the faerie you saw in my room."

"Is that why you have him locked up?" I ask. "Because he found out about Foster?"

She nods. "He found out during one of our missions to the fey realm. So, I bound him to me with a binding spell, then locked him in my room." She lets go of my hands with an exhausted sigh. "But it's not a long-term solution."

Gabe places a hand on her shoulder. "Sweetie, we'll figure something out."

"I know," Emaline whispers. "I'm just worried; that's all." She lowers her hands. "You know as well as I do that Kash will use Foster's powers to benefit him. And anything that benefits Kash will cause harm to our world."

"I promise everything will be fine." Gabe pulls her against his chest and hugs her.

Emaline clutches him, her eyes glazing over with ice. The temperature begins to drop, causing goosebumps to sprout on my arms.

"Come on." Max takes ahold of my hand. "Let's give my parents a moment, okay?"

I let Max lead me to the ledge of the podium. Then Holden moves up beside me and threads his fingers through my other hand while Hunter stands behind me.

Crowded. That's the word that comes to mine as I

peer left to right then over my shoulder. When my gaze collides with Hunter's, a smirk plays at his lips.

"There's no need to be nervous, little human." He winks at me. "We'll take good, *good* care of you."

I blink at him. Did he just call me *little human?*

"Good gods, Hunter," Holden mumbles. "You don't need to hit on everyone."

"I don't," Hunter replies without taking his eyes off me. "I only hit on the pretty ones."

I roll my eyes.

Hunter's smirk widens. "You know, I think you have some very fun potential in you, if we could just get you to let it out a bit more. I bet it'd help if we cracked through that invisible wall you have around you. Or well, break open that tiny crack in it."

My brows pull together. "What wall?"

He traces his palm in a circular motion in front of my face. "A few humans have invisible walls around them, or barriers, as I like to call them. But they're basically invisible walls that protect creatures like me from seeing someone's true self. A lot of creatures have them, but they've had them put around them purposefully and by magic, while human walls are usually created by traumatic, emotional experiences. It's a defense mechanism that few possess. And I'd say you should be proud to have a wall around you, but I'm concerned about what experiences created it and what caused the crack in it."

"I really don't know." Sure, my life hasn't always been sunshine and rainbows, but nothing traumatic happened to me. Well, except for ... "Maybe it's because my parents disappeared."

He shakes his head, his gaze scrolling from my feet to the top of my head. "The wall around you is very old. Maybe even as old as you are."

Confusion webs through me. "As far as I know, the only traumatic thing that's happened to me is my parents disappearing." Well, and the day I became aware that I had powers, but that part won't pass my lips.

Dammit, this is so frustrating! Why can't I say anything about my powers?

Hunter studies me closely, which causes heat to sprinkle across my skin. "Maybe you've forgotten what happened to you."

"How could I forget something traumatic?" I point out. "Those types of things usually stick with you."

"Not necessarily." He contemplates something before stepping back and launching himself over the edge of the podium, landing gracefully in the grass.

I glance between Max and Holden, who are looking at me with a hint of perplexity. "So, if Hunter can see this invisible wall around me, then I'm assuming you guys have some sort of powers not related to your elements."

Max and Holden trade a look then chuckle.

Heat creeps across my cheeks. *Are they making fun of me?*

"Don't worry; we're not making fun of you," Max says, as if reading my mind. "We've just never been around a human who knows about our world, so we didn't realize how entertaining these sorts of questions could be."

"And to answer your question," Holden says. "Yes, we do have powers that aren't related to our elements. We actually have a lot of different powers."

"Like what?" I cross my fingers, hoping they can't actually read minds. Although, there have been a couple of times when I wondered that, so ...

What if they can?

"Like being able to create portals." Holden hitches his thumb at the rainbow portal.

"Or like being extremely graceful and strong." To prove his point, Max picks me up and leaps off the edge of the podium before I can even take my next breath.

I barely feel the impact as he lands weightlessly in the grass.

"Wow," I breathe out, clutching the front of his shirt.

Grinning, he lowers my feet to the ground. "And there's plenty more where that came from." He spins on his heels and starts across the field in the direction Easton, Foster, and Hunter took off in, light orbs twirling around him.

I start to follow him when Holden drops down beside me.

"Are you okay?" he asks.

I nod, tucking a lock of hair behind my ear. "Yeah, I'm fine. Why?"

"Because this—this world, our powers—it can be a lot to take in."

"I'm fine," I assure him. But, am I? I'm not sure I know the answer to that.

Offering me a small smile, he pulls me with him as he starts across the field. "My brothers and I haven't ever been around a human who knows about our powers, so I'm guessing there's going to be a lot of showing off." The orbs of light magnetize toward him, but he doesn't seem to notice, his gaze welded to mine. "If you get uncomfortable at any time, just say so, okay? Don't let them do things to you that make you uncomfortable."

Worry crawls through me. Just what sort of things does he think they're going to do to me?

"They'd never hurt you," he promises, as if sensing my dread. "That I can promise you."

I hate to ask, but I need to know. "Does that statement apply to Foster, too?"

He nods with zero hesitation. "Foster is complicated, but he'd never hurt you. In fact, I think if he could, he'd like you."

"You make it sound like he has to hate me."

"He doesn't have to, but it's probably for the better. It always is." He doesn't elaborate, leaving me to wonder what he meant.

Leaving me to wonder a lot of things.

CHAPTER 14

"So, what exactly is this place called?" I ask after a few minutes of silence have drifted by between Holden and me.

Max is walking farther ahead, playing with the orbs of light. And, by playing, I mean that, every so often, he plucks a green one from the air and tosses it around like a baseball.

Green, just like his eyes and his magical light powers. I doubt that's a coincidence.

"We call this place The In-Between," Holden says as a golden orb of light lands on his shoulder. "But it's basically the place that links all the worlds."

It takes me a gulp or two to process his words. "So, what world are we going to now?"

"Our world." He pets the light with his fingertips. "Also known as Elemental."

"Just how many worlds are there?"

"More than even I know about." He gives me a sidelong glance. "I know it's a little overwhelming, but when you start going to the academy, you'll learn all about our world."

"Are all humans that go there aware of your powers?"

He shakes his head, collecting the light in his hand. "No. Actually, most of them don't know about us."

"But, how do you keep it a secret from them?"

He winks at me. "With magic."

"Oh."

God, this is so much to take in. Powers. Worlds. Orbs of light that act like pets.

"What are these light thingies anyway?" I point at the ball of light in his hand.

Smiling, he sticks his hand out toward me with the light resting in his palm. "This is what we refer to as essences. They exist only in The In-Between and, like our eyes, their color represents their power."

"So, they have the same powers as you guys?"

"Yes. Only, they never connected to a body."

"Connected to a body ...?" My confusion morphs

into shock. "Wait. Are you saying these things are what create people ...? Creatures like you?"

He nods, somewhat amused. "Although, not all of them will connect to a body. Some will always just roam The In-Between. Those we refer to as wild essences."

I glance curiously at the wild essence in his hand. "What does it feel like when you hold it?"

Pressing his lips together, he moves his hand in my direction again. "Touch it and find out."

"Will it ...? Can it hurt me?"

"No. Wild essences are as pure as untainted souls. I'm not sure if you'll actually feel anything since you're human, but I'm curious to find out."

It seems as if I should be afraid, but every single part of me is begging to touch the orb of light. So, like a magnet to metal, my fingers drift forward, the tips slipping through the light. A wave of heat and iciness courses through me, then a gust of wind kicks up, blowing through my hair and across my skin. Seconds later, the clouds begin to shower rain as lightning bolts zap and thunder booms, rumbling the ground.

"What the hell?" Holden peers up at the sky.

I gasp as electric energy surges through my veins, and Holden's attention whips to me as rays of light swarm around me, like a multicolored tornado.

"Hold perfectly still," Holden whispers as the rays of light eddy around me.

"Are they going to hurt me?" I whisper, my voice shaky.

"No, they're drawn to you." A crease forms at his brows. "Sky, is there any way you could have powers?"

I swallow hard, willing the words to leave my lips. But again, I remain silent.

The crease between his brows deepens. "Sky, can you hear me?"

I nod. "Yeah."

He surveys me over. "Can you not talk about something?" When I say nothing, he nibbles on his bottom lip. "If you think you have some sort of powers, nod your head."

I attempt to do just that, but my head won't budge. Frustrated, I ball my hands into fists. The movement captures his attention.

"You can't talk about it, can you?" he asks, frowning.

"I ... Why ... can't I?" I manage to strain out.

"I'm not sure." He taps his finger against his lips. "There've been a couple of instances when elemental protectors had spells cast on them to keep their identity and powers hidden. Usually, though, it's because they did something illegal and wanted to hide from the council. I know my grandparents did it once when they were younger, but that was to conceal that they were elemental enchanters ..." His eyes abruptly widen. Then his gaze travels across all the orbs of light whirling around me in a colorful stream. "Oh fuck." He snatches ahold of my hand and drags me back in the direction we just came from.

"What's going on?" I ask as I stumble after him.

He doesn't answer, taking longer strides, and I damn near eat dirt as I struggle to keep up with him. Finally, he scoops me up in his arms, and then we're moving so fast that the sky, trees, and light around us become nothing but blurs of colors.

Before I know it, we're back on the podium. Emaline and Gabe are still there but look as if they were about to leave.

"What's wrong?" Gabe asks immediately as Holden rushes up with me in his arms.

"All the essences are drawn to her," Holden hisses. "I think she might be an elemental enchanter."

Hearing him say the words aloud causes adrenaline to soar through me.

"*What?*" they simultaneously say, their eyes bulging as they gape at me.

"And she can't talk about it," Holden adds, "which means someone went through an awful lot of trouble to keep her powers a secret."

"But," Emaline sputters, "it can't be possible. Her parents are human."

"Unless they're not her real parents," Gabe states, avoiding my gaze.

Wait. *What?*

"Th-They're my parents," I sputter. "I know they are."

His eyes convey pity. "I know you've been through a lot lately, and this is probably the last thing you want to deal with, but humans can't have children with elemental powers. It's just not possible. And an elemental enchanter ..." He shakes his head. "They almost always come from a line of very powerful elemental protectors."

"Maybe my parents had powers and you just didn't know it?" I say. "I mean, no one knows about me ... Well, until now."

Gabe and Emaline exchange an unreadable look, then Gabe cautiously says, "Maybe." But I can tell he doesn't believe it.

My heart sinks in my chest. What if what they're saying is true? What if my entire life has been a lie?

"We need to get her out of here." Holden says with urgency.

"Why? Foster's here, and he's one, so ..." I'm so lost.

"It was odd enough that headquarters requested you come with us today," Holden tells me cautiously.

"Which means if someone knows what she is, this could be a setup." Gabe shakes his head with his jaw set tight. "I should've suspected it the moment I got the message."

Emaline places her hand on his arm. "Honey, you couldn't have known. None of us suspected she had powers."

"All the extra storms make sense now." Holden stares down at me with the strangest look on his face.

I become hyperaware he's still carrying me. "You can put me down if you want."

Strands of hair fall into his eyes as he shakes his head. "Nah, I'll carry you through the portal." He looks at Gabe. "So, what're we going to do?"

Gabe glances at the trees, the portal, me, then at Holden. "Take her back to the house. We'll find your brothers and send them back. Then your mother and I will go to headquarters."

"You think it's safe?" Holden asks, his arms tensing around me.

Gabe wavers. "I'm not sure, which is why we'll go to Gabby first. She'll be able to give us a sense of what's going on. We'll make our next decision based on that."

Worry crams Holden's expression. "Just be safe, okay?"

"Of course." Gabe forces a smile.

Holden sighs, striding across the podium toward the rainbow portal.

Guilt weighs down on my chest. If something happens to them, it'll be my fault.

Before I can verbalize my feelings, though, Holden jumps into the portal and rainbow light swallows us up.

CHAPTER 15

After Holden transports us through the portal and back to the Everettsons' living room, he sets me down on the sofa. "Stay here. I'll be right back." Then he spins on his heels and strides out of the room.

My palms are sweating and my pulse is soaring as I process everything I discovered over the last day. Powers. Paranormals. Me being some rare creature. That my parents might not actually be my real parents. How is this possible?

I'd probably be more in shock if I hadn't already been dealing with my powers for most of my life. While some of what I just learned is frightening—and frustrating, if it turns out my parents aren't my real parents—I also feel a trace of relief that, after all these years, I'm finally starting to understand why I can make lightning and fires ignite from out of nowhere, why I can sometimes start flashfloods, why light bulbs burst when I get angry. I've spent years believing I was crazy. Years thinking, if I really did have powers, I was the only one in the world who did.

"All right, I want to try a couple of things," Holden announces as he returns to the room. He has a small, leather bag in his hand and his sleeves are rolled up.

"What sort of things?" I dubiously eyeball the leather bag that looks an awful lot like an old-school doctor bag.

"Nothing bad. I promise." He sinks down onto the edge of the coffee table and opens the bag. "I want to see if I can get that invisible wall around you down. If I can, it might allow you to talk about your powers. It's got a tiny crack in it already, but we can use that to our advantage. Although, I'm curious what caused the crack."

"I have no idea." I pause. "You think this wall is what's restraining me from talking about... Well, you know?"

"It could be." He retrieves a thick, leather-bound book from the bag. "It could be a spell, though. If that's the case, we're going to need to bring in an elemental witch."

"Is that like a normal witch?" I pause as what he said sinks in. "Wait ... Witches exist?"

"Everything exists." He fans through the pages of the book. "But elemental witches are a bit different from normal witches. Where normal witches gain their powers from spells, elemental witches' powers come directly from the elements."

"So wind, fire, water, and ice," I list the elements I've heard about so far. "Are there any more elements?"

His throat muscles work as he swallows hard. "There's one more ... Darkness."

"I'm guessing from your tone that darkness isn't a good element?"

An uneven exhale eases from his lips. "Our history is filled with wars and dark periods caused by the elemental protectors of darkness. There's something about controlling darkness and being connected to it that makes a lot of them almost insane. It doesn't help that darkness is linked to dark magic, which is the most evilest form of magic."

"Do ...? Um ..." I nervously wet my chapped lips. "Elemental enchanters have all the elements, right? So that includes darkness?"

He nods. "Don't worry, though. Even though darkness is a part of you, elemental enchanters are known for doing more good than evil. And usually, they only cause evil when forced by the hand of another."

"Oh." I can't help thinking of Foster and the unkindness he's shown toward me.

"Foster isn't as cruel as he comes off. There's just a lot to being an elemental enchanter, which you'll learn about soon. That is, if I'm correct about you being one." He returns to skimming through the book.

Again, it's as though he can read my mind.

"You don't have mind-reading abilities, do you?" I ask while observing him closely.

His eyes crinkle around the corners as he chuckles. "No, but I can read people fairly well. You're a bit more complicated, though, with that wall around you." He sets the book down on the table and cracks his knuckles. "Hopefully, I can get it down so that can change."

"Yeah, I'm not sure I want you to be able to read me clearly." I anxiously eyeball his hands as flames spark from his fingertips.

"Don't worry; I can teach you how to block out elemental protectors, like me, who possess the gift of seeing. But we do need to get that wall down so we can see what's hidden behind it, okay?"

I nod, but my stomach ravels in knots. "Okay."

"Good. Now, I need you to hold still, and if at any time you feel like my powers are burning you, let me know, okay?" He waits for me to nod then glances down at the opened book. He skims over a page before looking at me again. Then he moves his hands toward my wrists. "Remember, let me know if it burns," he says as he brushes his fingertips over my skin, causing sparkly warmth to tingle up my arms and swim through my veins.

He examines my expression closely. "Feel anything?"

"It feels sparkly, but I've felt like this before when you touched me."

"Good. That's good." Sucking in a breath, he lays his palms on my arms.

The warmth intensifies, but not in a painful way. In fact, it feels good. Really, really good.

"Does it still feel sparkly?" he asks, and I nod, fighting the urge to close my eyes. "If it doesn't burn, then you for sure have elemental powers. But I still can't tell for sure."

"The wall's still up?"

"Yeah ..." He glances at the book again. "We might need more energy."

"More than what's pouring through my body now?" I choke out.

His gaze darts to mine, and then he hastily withdraws his hands from my arms. "Was I hurting you?"

"No, but it's ..." *Fucking weird and kind of wonderful.* Yeah, I'm not about to say that aloud. "Intense ... But not in a bad way."

He hesitantly places his palms back on my arms. "I have an idea, but we need my brothers here for it. Especially Foster, since he has the most power."

"What sort of idea?" Apprehension drips into my tone.

He doesn't get the chance to answer since the rest of the Everettson brothers come barreling through the portal.

Porter is the first to materialize, with Hunter right behind him. Then Max is next, Easton is second to last, with Foster hanging out near the back, appearing as irritated as he was the last time I saw him.

Porter takes one look at Holden and me sitting with our knees touching, Holden's hands on my arms, and his brow cocks up. "What'd we miss?"

Holden releases my arms and rises to his feet. "Mom and Dad didn't fill you in?"

Porter shakes his head, his gaze bouncing between Holden and me. "They just told us there was an emergency and we needed to get back to the house. That you and Sky would be here and could fill us in on everything."

All five of them glance between Holden and me.

Holden glances at me, and I shrug. "You know what's going on better than I do," I point out. "Honestly, I feel completely fucking lost."

"I know ... I was just ..." Holden glances worriedly

in Foster's direction then looks back at me. "I'm trying to figure out the best way to break the news to everyone."

Great, I have a feeling he thinks Foster is going to be upset that I might have the same powers as him.

"Come on, brother; just spit it out." Hunter motions for Holden to get a move on while plopping down on the sofa. "I'm sure whatever it is can't be that bad."

Again, Holden sneaks a glance at Foster.

Foster notices this time, and his brows furrow. "What's up? Why do you keep looking at me like that?"

Holden scratches the back of his neck. "Well, while we were in The In-Between, in the essences' field, I talked Sky into touching an essence."

"Really?" Intrigue sparkles in Hunter's eyes. "What happened? No, let me guess. It bit her?" His eyes glint mischievously. "I know I would."

Max rolls his eyes then winds around the table and takes a seat next to me. "I'm guessing a little essence bite isn't what caused Mom and Dad to make everyone return home."

"Nothing bit me," I stress, fidgeting with the leather bands on my wrists.

"That could be changed right now. All you have to do is say the word." Easton grins as I glare at him.

Then he flops down on a chair and kicks his feet up onto the coffee table. "I, for one, am glad we got to come home—whatever the reason." He kicks off his boots. "I really wasn't up to dealing with the council today."

"Nobody ever is." Max reclines back on the sofa and fixes his gaze on Holden. "So, are you going to tell us what happened?"

Again, Holden's gaze strays to Foster.

Foster narrows his eyes at him. "Stop giving me weird looks and just spit it out."

"You might want to sit down first," Holden tells him warily.

Foster crosses his arms. "No thanks. I'm good right here."

Jeez, is it really that big of a deal? So what if I'm an elemental enchanter?

Holden must think it's a big deal, though, because he frowns.

"Can you at least move away from the portal?"

Blowing out a frustrated exhale, Foster strides across the room and plops down on the end table near the sofa next to Porter. "All right, spill it."

Holden rakes his hands through his hair. "When Sky touched the essence, every single essence in the field swarmed up to her." Shocked silence sweeps across the room, but Holden presses on. "So, Mom,

Dad, and I think that ... well, with all the essences drawn to her ... she might be—"

"Like me," Foster finishes flatly, his expression neutral as he rises to his feet. "Awesome. Glad you dragged that out for an unnecessary amount of time." With that, he storms out of the room.

Holden pinches the bridge of his nose. "Will someone please go get him and convince him to come back here? I need his help trying to get this wall around Sky down."

"Can't you do it without him?" The last thing I want is to let Foster put his hands on my arms like Holden did. "Because I doubt he's going to help."

"He will." Max smiles tightly at me. "He's just ... He's thought for years that he's the only one of his kind, and it's going to take him some time to adjust to the reality that he's not."

My gaze skims across the five of them. Holden appears worried. So does Max. And Porter, Hunter, and Easton are staring at the doorway that Foster disappeared through, tension flowing off them.

"You guys aren't telling me something," I say. "Is it bad that there're two elemental enchanters?" Or is Foster just being a brat?

Maybe he likes being unique, and now that he's not, they're all worried he's going to throw a fit.

"No, it's not a bad thing." Max rotates in the chair

to face me. "It is a bit dangerous, though, to be an elemental enchanter. Not that I want to frighten you, but you need to understand that, because of your immense powers, your kind are always at risk for being ... hunted."

"Holden explained a little bit of that to me." I hug my arms around myself as chills break out across my skin. "So, how does Foster stay safe?"

"He has us." Hunter winks at me, but the typical glimmer in his eyes isn't present.

"I'm not going to be, like, restricted to the house or something, am I?" Not that I'd ever agree to that. In fact, I still plan on continuing with my plans of leaving when I graduate. And I need to visit Nina and Gage soon. "I don't want my life to change."

"You're not going to be restricted to the house," Max reassures me, sliding his arm along the back of the sofa behind me. "But not everything's going to be the same. You'll have to learn to control your powers ..." He pauses, his forehead bunching. "Wait. How long have you had your powers anyway?"

I stare at him, my lips refusing to allow me to answer.

"She can't talk about anything directly related to her powers," Holden explains, resting his arms on his knees. "I think the wall around her might have some magic laced into it, keeping her from doing so."

"Meaning someone went through a lot of trouble to keep what she is a secret," Porter says, his gaze glued to me. "Your parents maybe?"

Again, I can't answer. And not just because my lips won't cooperate, but because I honestly don't know the answer.

When I make no effort to respond, Holden yanks his fingers through his hair. "We really need to get this wall down. I've already tried, but I think I need more power."

"Well, there're six of us. That should be enough." Max points at the doorway. "East, go get Fost."

Easton arches a brow. "You think he's going to listen to *me*?"

Max presses him with a firm look. "Make him understand the bigger picture."

"Fine." Easton pushes to his feet and hurries across the room, casting a weird glance at me before walking out.

"You know it's not going to be that easy, right?" Porter tells Max as he props his boot-clad foot onto his knee. "It's going to take Fost a while to get used to this."

"I know." Max roughly drags his fingers through his hair. "But, right now, he needs to suck it up. He can have his meltdown later."

Thunder abruptly booms, and the entire house quivers.

"Well, I think Easton just repeated your message to him," Hunter quips to Max then flashes a grin in my direction. "Unless you're doing that?"

"Nope, that's not me." I'm surprised I can say those words aloud, seeing as it has to do with my powers. Then again, it's sort of me denying I'm using my powers, so ...

I'm so damn confused, among a million other things, and that confusion only magnifies when Easton returns to the room with a pissed off looking Foster in tow.

Seriously, what's the deal with this guy? Why does he seem to hate me? Because he finds me repulsive? So what? That doesn't give him the right to treat me like shit.

"So, what the hell are we doing?" Foster grumbles as he crosses his arms.

"We're going to try to get this wall around Sky down. But I think it's going to take all our powers, especially yours." Holden approaches Foster then leans in and lowers his voice, whispering something to him.

Foster absorbs his words, his gaze skating in my direction.

Awesome. They're talking about me. That's okay,

though. At this point in my life, I'm used to guys being jerks toward me. At least, that's what I try to convince myself. But the truth is, having Foster hate me is going to suck big time since we're living under the same roof.

"Fine," Foster says after Holden is done whispering to him.

Holden nods, gives him a pat on the shoulder, then moves back and turns to address the room. "So, I've been looking through Mom and Dad's book of secret spells, and there's one that suggests our powers can break a blocking spell."

"You think that's what she's got around her?" Porter asks.

Holden gives a wavering nod. "It's my best guess."

"I think you're probably right." Max tosses a glance at me. "I noticed she was unreadable the first time I met her, which I thought was pretty weird. Since I thought she was human, though, I didn't think it could be a blocking spell. Now that we know she's probably not human, I'm betting that's what it is. I also know that disintegrating blocking spells can be complicated and sometimes nearly impossible."

"I know." Holden stuffs his hands into his back pockets. "But it can't hurt to try."

"I don't know about that," I chime in. "Disintegrating anything sounds kind of dangerous."

"You should get used to danger," Foster says in a

neutral tone that throws me off a bit. *Where'd the snippy Foster go?* "Our kind are always in danger of something." A strange, horrifyingly puzzled look flashes across his face before he looks away from me and swallows hard. "It's what killed our grandparents."

Fear lashes through me. "What happened to them?"

"Let's save that story for another time," Holden says before Foster can reply. "Right now, we need to try to get that wall down." He collects the opened book from the table and hands it to Max, tapping the top of the page. "That's what I want to try."

I lean over to get a look, but Max is already slanting forward and handing the book to Porter. After Porter reads the page, he gives the book to Hunter.

"It could work," Porter says. "But we need to be careful that we don't overload her with our powers."

"Elemental enchanters are made to absorb powers," Max reminds him, resting back on the sofa.

"Is that what you guys were doing to Foster in the woods?" I ask as the memory of them all blasting their powers into him flashes through my mind.

Holden nods. "Because elemental enchanters have so much power, my family and I go into the woods at least once a week so he can practice using them without being seen."

"Why did you even go into the woods anyway?" Hunter asks me with curiosity sparkling in his eyes.

I shrug. "Because I saw you and Holden go in there, and you didn't look like you were going to play baseball."

"So, you thought we were doing what?" he asks, unzipping his hoodie.

I shrug again. "I wasn't sure, but between the weird conversations I overheard, the strange screaming from last night, seeing Max in the backyard with his eyes glowing, and the eyeballs in the fridge, I had a feeling something was ... off about you guys. And then I saw you and Holden walk through that rippling, clear wall and into the trees ..." I pause. "What are the eyeballs for anyway?"

"Holden and Hunter's science experiments." Porter tells me the same thing he did last night. "I wasn't lying about that."

"Oh." I open my mouth to ask what sort of experiments, but Holden speaks first.

"We should probably get this spell started," he says. "The sooner we can get that wall down, the sooner we can find out what Sky really knows and maybe even why the wall was put up to begin with."

They all nod in agreement.

"Are you sure this is safe?" I question.

Holden nods. "It'll be similar to what I just did to

you earlier, only it'll be all of us. And like I said before, if at any time you feel too hot or too cold or too anything, just say so and we'll stop."

"You were nervous before when you first put your hands on me," I remind him.

"I know, but you handled my powers just fine." He offers me what appears to be a genuine smile. "I promise we won't let anything happen to you."

"Our parents would kick our asses if we did," Easton adds, standing up and tossing the book onto the coffee table. "So, how exactly are we going to do this?" he asks Holden. "Just stand in a circle around her?"

"I think that'd be best, but maybe ..." Reluctance creeps across Holden's face. "Maybe have Foster stand in the circle with her."

I grind my teeth, wanting to protest, but since I have no clue what they're about to do, I decide not to.

Holden glances over his shoulder at Foster. "Is that okay with you?"

Foster lifts a shoulder. "I guess." He stands in the same place for a flicker of a second then walks up to me and sticks out his hand.

I should be cooperative—I usually am—but this guy has gotten under my skin. So, instead of taking his hand, I scoot to the side of the sofa, stand up, and wind around him.

"Where should I stand?" I direct my question at Holden.

Holden's gaze shifts between Foster and me, then he sighs and points at a wide area on the other side of the room. "Over there works."

I walk over to the spot he pointed at, and the rest of them join me, creating a circle around me. All except for Foster who moves in front of me, standing so he's facing me.

"You're going to have to touch me if this is going to work," Foster says, pushing up the sleeves of his hoodie.

I glance at Holden for confirmation.

He gives me a nod. "He's telling the truth."

Blowing out a breath, I return my attention to Foster, who has his hand out. I make no move to take it, though.

"Stop looking at me like I have cooties," he gripes.

"Maybe you do," I retort. "And when I touch you, they'll leak all over me."

He rolls his tongue in his mouth, fighting back what looks like a smile. But it's hard to say for sure since I'm fairly certain I've never seen him smile.

"I'll tell you what. If you take my hand, I'll try not to spread my cooties to you." He urges his hand at me.

"You better." I know I'm being ridiculous, but he's been such a jerk to me. Plus, I'm feeling very stressed out right now. But, knowing I don't have another choice, I suck it up and place my hand in his.

Nothing could prepare me for what happens next.

I gasp as sparks of electricity surge from him and crackle across my arm. Foster's eyes illuminate as they widen, lightning-blue light piercing across the room.

"What the hell?" I hear one of the Everettson brothers say, but the howling wind makes it hard to figure out who spoke.

Water pours through the room and splatters across the floor. Light bulbs burst, snowflakes flurry from somewhere, and a fire erupts in the fireplace.

I should pull away—whatever is happening between Foster and me is going to end up destroying the house—but the power running through my veins ... the warmth ... the sparkling ... it feels so wonderful.

"Good gods," Foster breathes out, his chest rising and crashing as he gapes at me. "I've never felt anything ... like ... this—"

He gasps as a lightning bolt crashes through the room and zaps the floor right between us.

We both stumble back, the chaos settling as ours hands separate.

Then my eyes roll into the back of my head and everything goes dark.

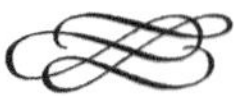

CHAPTER 16

Darkness everywhere. Calling to me. Begging for me to own it.

I want to let it wrap around me. Want it to become a part of me.

"Can you hear me?" darkness whispers. "If you can, just give in. We need a queen ..."

I'm not sure what queen it's talking about, but I find myself reaching farther into the darkness, letting it take me away—

My eyelids snap open, and I bolt upright, panting for air as I frantically glance around, half-expecting to see nothing but darkness. Then I relax a drop when I see black and purple walls.

I'm in my bedroom at the Everettsons' house. I'm safe. There's no darkness.

But, how did I end up here? The last thing I can recall is being in the living room ... the lightning ... Foster. And what was that dream? Why did darkness call to me? And what queen was it talking about?

Climbing out of the bed, I check myself over to make sure the lightning that struck between Foster and me didn't do any damage. My skin is smooth, not a single injury evident, although the hem of my shirt looks singed.

I really need some answers.

Sweeping my fingers through my tangled hair, I make my way out of my room and down the hallway. The atmosphere is quiet until I reach the top of the stairs. Then I hear voices floating up from the living room.

I stop at the top of the stairs as Holden says, "So, the council just wanted to call her in because they think she's a human who knows about our world and wanted to make sure we had everything under control?"

"That's what they told us," Emaline replies.

Some of the tension I've been carrying unwinds from my muscles at the sound of her voice. Holden seemed worried when we last saw Emaline and Gabe, as if something bad might happen to them.

"We're not sure if they were telling the truth,

though. You know how corrupt everything's gotten back in our world. It's hard to trust anyone these days," Gabe says then sighs. "I'm going to look into it some more. Until then, we need to keep an extra eye on Sky."

Easton snickers. "I don't think that'll be a problem for Foster."

I hear a *whack*. Then ...

"Fuck off, man," Foster growls. "You don't know shit about this."

"Language," Emaline scolds.

"Sorry," Foster mutters. "I'm just a little stressed out. What happened in the living room with her ... that was ... intense."

"Intense in a good way?" Max asks curiously. "From what it looked like, I'm guessing so."

When Foster doesn't answer right away, Hunter chimes in. "Bro, it's okay to admit you liked it. Despite what you've had to tell yourself for the last several years, it's actually not a bad thing to like a girl."

Wait ... Are they talking about *me*?

I promptly shake my head. Hell no. There's no way Foster likes me.

Of course, the next thing Foster says gives me one scenario where he could. A scenario that makes my stomach churn and frustration roar through me.

"I understand that," Foster replies quietly, his tone crammed with fear and agony. "But it's hard. I spent most of my life believing I was the only elemental enchanter, and that I will never be able to get close enough to anyone to have a romantic relationship—at least, not without my powers killing them—so I shut almost everyone out." He releases a shaky breath. "Now I find out I'm not the only elemental enchanter, and that I can possibly have what I thought I never could ..."

I back away, not wanting to hear the rest, my mind racing as I rush back to my room.

What Foster just said ... Does it mean only an elemental enchanter can date another elemental enchanter? If that's so, then that means ...

I slip inside my room, shut the door, and yank my fingers through my hair. "Goddammit! How did every-thing get so messed up? Why did I have to come here? I just want to go home." Tears of frustration flood my eyes, and the sky weeps with me. "I need to get out of here ... take a break, get some answers," I whisper as I hurry into the closet to grab a bag.

As I'm packing, I dig out my phone, glad to see it's working again.

I text Nina, begging her to come get me. She replies almost instantly.

Nina: I can leave now. Just send me the address.

I do what she asks then finish packing, taking a couple of outfits, my toiletries, and a couple of the joints Gage gave me. I'm not running away or anything. I just need a break. I also want to go to the storage unit where my parents' stuff is and see if perhaps there's anything in there that'll give me some answers as to what the hell is going on.

I should probably go tell Emaline I'm leaving, especially since I'm supposed to be starting school tomorrow, but I can't seem to bring myself to face any of them right now, not after what I just heard. So, like a coward, I sneak downstairs to the back door, passing through the kitchen on my way so I can get Emaline's phone number off the iPad. That way, I can text her and let her know where I've gone. From what I can tell, the Everettson family is still discussing the issue at hand as I sneak out the back door.

I feel awful for bailing. Sure, the entire situation is fucked up, but most of them have treated me decently. All except Foster and sometimes Easton.

Foster, the only other elemental enchanter in the world.

The only person I can ever have a relationship with.

Fuck, what if that's true?

That question repeatedly streams through my mind as I hurry out the front gate and wait for Nina by the side of the road.

The sky grows dark as time passes, and rain drizzles from the clouds, soaking through my jacket. But I remain standing out in the storm, without shelter, strangely content with the rain. Well, that is until I get the strangest feeling I'm being watched.

The rain is coming down too hard to see much around me, and as the feeling increases, I debate going back into the house. Right as I'm turning to go back in, though, Nina pulls up.

Sighing in relief, I climb into the passenger seat.

"Holy shit, this is where you live now?" she asks as I shut the door.

I nod, fastening my seatbelt. "Yep, this is home sweet home," I reply dryly.

"It's gorgeous," she says, unable to tear her eyes off the house. "Seriously, what's it like living here?"

I peek over at the Everettsons' home, only one word coming to mind when I think about the last couple of days. "Chaotic." I sink back in the seat. "Let's get out of here before they realize I'm gone."

It takes her a raindrop of a second before she drives forward into the night.

Strangely, the farther away I get from the house,

the more unsettled I feel, as if some unseen force is begging me to go back. But I'm not ready to face any of them yet. Not until I process what I just heard. So, I ignore the inkling. Just like I ignore the lightning in the sky. Lightning not being caused by me.

I feel like a fugitive on the run as I cruise down the highway with Nina. But I shouldn't feel this way. I had ever right to take off after learning that Foster is the only guy I can be with. At least that's what I keep telling myself. But I feel this silent pull, whispering for me to return to the house.

No, I need a break. Need to clear my head.

"So ... do you want to talk about what happened?" Nina asks me as she steers down the highway.

The windshield wipers work to keep the rain off, but the storm is coming down so heavily that visibility is limited.

I reach to turn up the air. "It wasn't anything major," I lie. *Always lying. All the time.* "They're just jerks. Well, some of them are." Honestly, most of them aren't, but I don't know what else to tell her. "I just needed a break. Plus, they're really ... weird."

She laughs softly, cranking up the defroster as the windows fog up. "Sky, you do realize you're weird, right? Not that I don't love you any less." She downshifts and slows down for a turn. "How could I when I'm just as big of a weirdo?"

"Yeah, I guess so." God, I hate lying. Will there ever be a time when I can just tell the truth? Tell her about my powers?

Doubtful, especially with the wall that's blocking me. Unless the wall is down now ... I'm unsure if the spell worked since I passed out.

"Cheer up, buttercup," she says when she notices my frown. "We're going to have fun tonight."

I eye her over suspiciously. "Wait ... You have that tone."

Her eyes glint mischievously. "What tone?"

"The one you get when you're about to do something potentially illegal and try to convince me to do it with you."

"Don't pretend like you actually care about doing illegal stuff."

"I don't to an extent." I frown as she grins. "What's going on?"

"Oh, nothing." Her grin suggests otherwise. "Gage and I are just having a little get-together. That's all."

"So, a party." Because Nina never has get-togethers. They're always parties.

She shoots me a playful, scolding look. "Don't pout. It's going to be fun. I promise."

"Why'd you guys decide to have one tonight?" I ask. "And what about school tomorrow?"

"Our school's on winter break right now, remember?"

"Crap, I forgot. The new school I'm starting isn't on break yet."

"They do get a winter break, though, right?" she asks, and I shrug. "Well, shit."

"You can say that again," I mumble, folding my arms over my chest.

"Well, shit." She smiles, and I can't help smiling a bit, too.

But the party has me on edge.

"So, who's all coming to the party? And are you having it at Gage's or your house?"

"It's at mine. My mom's out of town, so I thought: why not?" She shrugs, then glances at me. "Just a warning. It was already going on when I left, and things were getting a bit crazy." When my lips curve into a frown, she adds, "Dude, chill. We're going to have fun."

I put on a smile, but the truth is that I've never been into parties. There're always too many people there for my liking. And with the mood I'm in, I am betting I'm going to be a party pooper. Not that I'm ever the life of the party.

I guess I'll just have to suck it up. After all, Nina did drive all the way out to the Everettsons' house just to pick my ass up.

Speaking of the Everettsons ...

I dig out my phone, deciding to send Emaline a text now.

Me: Hey ... So, I'm not sure if you noticed I'm gone or not, but I just wanted to let you know that I left the house. With everything going on, I needed a break. This is just a lot to take in ...

I don't know what else to tell her, so I hit send then hold my breath and wait for a reply. Almost instantaneously, a message pings through.

Emaline: Sky, I know you're probably scared and upset, but I need you to come home right now. It's not safe for you to be wandering around alone.

Me: I'm not alone. I'm with my friends.

Emaline: Your friends aren't one of us, sweetie. If something happens, they can't protect you.

Me: Please just let me hang out with them for a couple of days. I promise I'll come back as soon as I clear my head.

And after I've gone through the stuff in the storage unit.

Emaline: Where are you right now?

Me: Heading to Nina's house. She's my best friend. I'm in her car right now, perfectly safe.

Emaline: Where does she live?

Me: In Honeyton.

Emaline: I need the address.

I pause. If I give her the address, is she going to come get me?

Me: Why?

Emaline: So I can send someone to pick you up. I know that's not what you want to hear, and I understand that you've been through a lot, but you need to come home right now.

Me: I have no home.

I type and send the words without really thinking, sadness clutching my chest.

Another message buzzes through.

Emaline: Oh sweetie, that's not true at all. I know this has to be hard—learning

what you learned after losing your parents —but I promise that, with time, things will get easier. And our home is your home.

As tears well in my eyes, I shove my phone into my pocket. Her kindness is making me too emotional, and the sky is reacting by pouring down more rain.

"Holy crap, this is some storm," Nina remarks, peering up at the sky through the windshield. "And it was clear skies when I left my house."

"Storms are pretty unpredictable." To most people anyway.

To me, they're the most predictable thing in my life right now.

BY THE TIME WE ARRIVE AT NINA'S HOUSE, IT'S nearing eleven o'clock at night and the party is in full swing. Nina's house, which is similar to the size of my old home, is crammed with people, most of which I know but rarely talk to. They are all dancing, drinking, laughing, and smoking. The place reeks like cigarettes and beer, and the air is laced with smoke so potent my eyes immediately water.

"I'm back!" Nina singsongs as we enter the kitchen.

Gage, who's sitting on the counter, chatting with a

red-headed girl who looks a year or two older than us, smiles at Nina. Then his smile morphs into a full-blown grin when his gaze lands on me.

"What the hell? I didn't know you were coming." He jumps off the counter and wraps his arms around me in a hug, smelling like pot and beer and everything that is Gage.

"Hey." I loop my arms around the back of his neck as he spins me around. "Didn't Nina tell you she was going to pick me up?"

He shakes his head, slanting back to meet my gaze. "She told me she was going to get a surprise, but that's it." He kisses my cheek. "Best surprise ever."

I chuckle, knowing he's drunk. "For sure."

After he steps away, he assesses me. "Something's off about you."

I instantly think of the wall around me. Could he be saying that because it's down now? But, if that's the case, then wouldn't he have been able to see it to begin with?

Is Gage not human?

That idea quickly evacuates my brain when he laughs and says, "Oh, I know why. It's because you're not drunk yet." He snags ahold of my hand and drags me over to the table that holds an array of drinks.

After he mixes me one, he pours a drink for

himself. "Cheers." He taps his cup against mine, and I can't help laughing as he spills some all over his boots and the floor.

Shrugging it off with a laugh, he downs a large mouthful then waits for me to do the same. Part of me doesn't want to drink, is worried that, with everything going on, I shouldn't. But when thunder rumbles from outside, reminding me of reality, I decide to hell with it and down a large gulp.

Once we've both finished our drinks, Gage tosses our cups into the garbage then glances around. "What should we do next?"

I look around at the rowdy crowd. "Where's Nina?"

Gage lifts his shoulders. "Probably up in one of the bedrooms with Logan."

I pull a face. "Grey's friend?"

Gage offers me an apologetic look. "Sorry, but you know how she can get."

"Yeah, she thinks with her vagina, not her head," I say, jolting as a loud boom of thunder reverberates through the house.

Since I'm slightly buzzed and feeling somewhat content, I'm surprised I'm setting off a storm. Maybe another drink will help. Or maybe ...

"You know, I brought a couple of those joints you

gave me," I tell Gage, knowing I might be heading down a path of self-destruction, but right now, I'm too confused, lost, worried, scared—a hundred different things—to care.

He points a finger at me, a devious smile curling at his lips. "I like the way you think."

I grin back, though I feel anything but happy. Still, I act the part as Gage and I go back to the extra bedroom and light up.

A few inhales in, and I'm feeling pretty numb inside, although the storm hasn't calmed down yet.

"So, what's life like at your new home?" Gage asks, passing me the joint.

We're stretched out on the bed with our feet in opposite directions, our heads side by side.

"It's ... weird." I take a hit and hand it back.

"Weird how?"

"I don't know ... Just weird."

"You're not making very much sense, hon." He rolls over onto his stomach with the joint pinched between his fingers and looks down at me. "They're not treating you shitty, are they?"

I shake my head. "No, not really. Most of them are nice. Well, except for Foster. But he's ... I don't know." I frown, or more like pout, when I realize I can't tell him much more than that.

Smoke snakes around his face as he studies me. "Did you ever figure out who that guy was that approached you yesterday? And why he gave you a blank card?"

I shake my head. Through all the craziness that has been happening, I completely forgot about that guy.

"Why do you ask?" I wonder, taking the joint from him.

He shrugs, then flips back onto his back. "I was just curious ... I mean, you act like these people you're living with are weird and that guy said that stuff about them ..." He shrugs, staring up at the ceiling.

My mind drifts back to when the guy had given me the card. He said the Everettsons weren't who I thought they were. He also said to call him when I wanted to know the truth, yet there wasn't anything on the card he gave me. Does he really know what the Everettsons are? Is he an elemental protector? Why single me out, though?

I recall how he noticed when my powers made the lights flicker.

Does he know what I am?

Crap, what if he does?

I need to look at the card again. Maybe I missed something the first time I glanced at it.

"I need to go get something out of my bag," I mutter, rolling off the bed.

Gage lifts his head, blinking at me. "What?"

"Nothing. I'll be right back." I motion for him to stay put, which he obliges, lying back down and taking another hit.

I stumble out of the room, my vision a bit blurry and time feeling a bit off, as if I'm moving in slow motion.

"Sorry," I apologize as I bump into someone. Then I hear an all-too-familiar laugh.

"Man, someone's out of it," Grey remarks, steadying me by the shoulders.

I sigh, so not in the mood to deal with him right now.

"Excuse me," I tell him, trying to squeeze by him, but he sidesteps, blocking my way.

When I glare at him, the corners of his lips curve upward.

"What're you doing here?" he asks. "I didn't think you were much of a partier."

His speculation is stupid because A). He doesn't know me very well. B). I'm not a partier right now. Just a girl at a party. And C) ...

I totally forgot where I was going with this.

Crap, I think I smoked too much.

"Can you please move out of my way?" I ask. "I need to go do something."

Ignoring me, he nibbles on his bottom lip. "You asked me to a dance once, right? When we were, like, in seventh or eighth grade?"

"That was a long time ago," I point out defensively. Although, if I weren't high, I'd probably get flustered.

"And if I remember correctly, I turned you down."

"Move out of my way," I grit out through my teeth, my anger trying to surface, but the haziness inside me stifles it.

He ignores me. "You know what? I'm feeling pretty generous tonight, so how about we have that dance?"

"Gag me." I don't mean to say the words aloud. They just sort of fall from my mouth.

A slow grin curls at his lips. "So, the little weirdo likes kinky shit, huh?"

Before I can fully comprehend what he said, he has me backed up against the wall and pinned between his arms. His breath reeks of vodka as he leans in, his lips an inch away from mine.

I peer around the empty hallway and panic. Gage is nearby, though, so if I shout, he'll probably come out here.

"Back off," I warn, preparing to knee him in the balls. "Seriously, back the fuck—"

He crashes his lips against mine as he steals my first kiss.

That asshole!

I move to knee him between the legs when a sharp zap nips across my skin.

Grey jerks back, his eyes wide, blue bolts of electricity crackling across his flesh.

"Holy shit," he breathes out, reaching his sparking fingers toward his lips.

I expect him to freak out, but instead, he growls and moves to slam his lips against mine again. I lift my fist, preparing to punch him, when he flies back against the opposite wall.

At first, I think maybe my powers did it, but then I hear a voice. A very annoying voice.

"Haven't you ever heard the term *no means no?*" Easton steps up beside Grey, crossing his arms and staring him down.

I blink a couple of times to be certain I'm seeing things correctly. Or maybe I'm hallucinating?

After a few more blinks, I realize that yes, Easton is here, along with Max and Foster. How they found me, I haven't a clue, other than maybe one of them has tracking powers or something.

I jut out my lip, pouting over the fact that they're

here. Foster is so the last person I want to see right now.

Foster glances at my jutted-out lip then presses his together, as if he's struggling not to smile. But then he quickly shakes his head, erasing the look.

"Are you okay?" he asks, his voice carefully controlled.

I don't respond, looking at Max instead. "Why are you guys here? And how did you find me?"

"We're here to get you. And we found you by tracking you ..." Max's brows knit. "Are you on something?"

I shake my head. "No ..."

He frowns in disbelief. "Your eyes are really bloodshot."

I waver. "I may be a little high, but it's not a big deal."

Foster inches toward me, his posture tense. "Do you realize how dangerous it is for you to be this out of it ..." He trails off as he glances down at Grey, whose eyes are droopy and his shoulders are slumped.

He looks completely dazed, as if he has no idea where he is or who he is.

"What did you guys do to him?" I ask, assuming Grey's suddenly incoherent state has to do with their powers.

"We'll explain in the car." Max reaches for my hand.

I step away from him. "I'm not going with you. I came here to take a break from ... everything."

Max sighs. "Sky, it's not safe for you to be wandering around by yourself."

"I'm not by myself. I have my friends," I point out. "And even if I was by myself, I've spent years being on my own, and so far, I've been fine."

Easton gives an insinuating look at Grey. "Clearly."

"That's not my fault," I hiss. "One of you guys did that to him."

"No, we didn't." Easton props his shoulder against the wall. "That was all you, lightning eyes."

"No ... there's no way I did ... *that*." I gesture at Grey.

Easton looks at me with pity. "You kissed him, right?"

"No," I say. When they silently stare me down, I add, "He tried to kiss me, and then ... well, there were these sparks ... But not the magical, that-was-an-awesome-kiss-that-rocked-my-world kind. It was really weird."

"I'm guessing you've never kissed anyone before," Easton says, his gaze glittering with curiosity.

I narrow my eyes at him. "Fuck off."

A grin spreads across his lips. "Damn, she's getting feistier by the second. I like it."

"Knock it off," Foster snaps, tossing Easton an icy look.

I think about what I overheard in the living room, how an elemental enchanter can only be with another elemental enchanter. So, does he think we're going to become a couple now? Because, yeah, no thank you.

"Screw you guys. I'm not going anywhere with you." I whirl around to bolt back to the bedroom Gage is in, but two steps forward and arms circle my waist.

"I'm sorry, but you don't have a choice." Foster pulls me against him.

"Leave me alone." I fling my weight forward, my skin crackling with electricity either from my power or his—I can't really tell.

"Not until you calm down and agree to go back with us," he says, tightening his arms around me. "Stop being such a brat."

"*I'm* the brat?" I laugh, the noise strained. "You're the one who's having a temper tantrum because you're not a special little snowflake anymore."

"That's not what that was about," he bites out, sounding pained.

"Sure it wasn't." Realizing I'm not going to be able to wiggle free on my own, I place my hand on his arm and try to channel the same power as when we touched in the living room.

His skin hisses, but that's about it. Talk about anti-climactic.

"Go ahead and try it," he breathes in my ear. "Now that I've felt your powers, I can control them—and my own—better."

I grimace, moving my hand off his arm. "I don't want to go back to you guys' house. It's not my house … and I …" Tears pool in my eyes, but I suck them back. "I just want my old life back. I didn't ask for this."

I loathe that I'm cracking apart in front of them, that I'm veering toward a meltdown, but I can't seem to regain control over my emotions.

"I know it's hard, and I understand you're probably scared and don't want this," Foster says, his tone softening, "but the reality is that you are an elemental enchanter, and if the wrong creature finds out about you, you could wind up dead. Or worse."

His words send a chill up my spine.

"What's worse than death?" I ask, tilting my head back to meet his gaze.

"I hope you never have to find out."

The worry in his tone makes me gulp.

Taking an unsteady breath, Foster releases me and

steps back, but stays close. "Now, please get your stuff so we can take you home."

Huh? Who would've thought he knew how to say please?

While I don't want to go back to their house, his words have scared me enough that I'm going to listen.

I turn toward him, my gaze skimming across Max and Easton, who are surprisingly not looking at me but staring at Foster, with weird, curious expressions.

"Can I at least stay here until I'm sober?" I ask none of them in particular. "I have a feeling your parents aren't going to be cool with me showing up like this." I gesture at my face and somehow manage to smack myself in the eye. "Ow."

Max smashes his lips together, but Easton doesn't even try to conceal his laughter, and Foster sinks his teeth into his bottom lip.

"That wasn't funny," I say, but then I chuckle because it sort of was. I press the heel of my hand to my eye. "I have a feeling that's going to hurt like a bitch in the morning."

"We'll put some ice on it tonight," Foster says, the word *we'll* making me cringe.

"I can put ice on it myself." I let a gradual exhale ease from my lips as he studies me way too intently. "Why are you looking at me like that?"

"Like what?" Foster questions, continuing to look at me the same way.

"Like ... I don't know." I shrug. "Like you're trying to kill me just by looking at me."

Easton snorts, and Foster glares at him. But Easton disregards the dirty look, his gaze remaining fixed on me.

"You'll have to excuse my brother," he says with a haughty grin. "He's a little out of practice."

My brows pull together. "With what?"

Foster blasts him with another nasty look. "East, I swear to the gods, if you don't shut up, I'm going to shove you in Max's trunk."

"The one in the attic?" I ask, recalling the locked trunk I stumbled across when I was up there.

Foster nods, eyeing me carefully. "You didn't open it, did you?"

"I doubt she'd be here if she did," Max tells him before I can reply. "And it's locked anyway."

Foster gives me a strange look. "Yeah, but she seems like the sort of girl who knows how to pick a lock."

"What's that supposed to mean?" I ask, crossing my arms.

"I don't know. You just seem like you're ..." He shrugs.

"I think he was trying to compliment you, lightning eyes," Easton says in an amused tone. "I'm not exactly sure how, though."

Foster's eyes shoot daggers at Easton. "You're really starting to get on my nerves."

"Oh, chill out. I'm just having some fun with the new bit of information we discovered earlier today," Easton tells Foster with a smirk. "Honestly, I never thought I was going to get a chance to tease you about your flirting skills, since you've never used them."

Foster pales, his eyes narrowing into slits, his arms hissing with blue sparks. "Shut up."

"East." A warning rings in Max's tone. "I think you'd better lay off this for now."

East's gaze descends to the sparks on Foster's arms, yet instead of looking worried, his smirk grows.

Foster lets out a low growl that sends a shiver rolling across my body, yet I have the strangest compulsion to reach out and brush my fingers along the sparks, to feel his power—

"There you are." Gage moves up beside me and drapes an arm across my shoulders. "I was seriously starting to worry you got lost ..." He trails off as he notes the three Everettson brothers then glances at me with his brow arched. "Why're they here?"

"I wasn't supposed to leave the house." I cast a discreet glance in Foster's direction and breathe in relief when I see that the sparks across his skin are no longer present.

The last thing I need is for Gage to see that and start asking questions. Then again, he might be so high I could probably convince him he's seeing things.

"Really?" The idea seems to greatly puzzle him. "The new parentals are that strict?"

I shrug. "Apparently."

Flicking a glance at the Everettson brothers, he leans in and whispers, "You want me to help you escape? We can go to my house and hang out there for a while."

I have no idea how, but I can feel Foster's gaze burning into me. Inside my chest, something sparks. The heat is a painful reminder of what I am. And as Grey starts to stir beside my feet, reality bitch-slaps me across the face.

"I actually think I better go back," I mutter with a sigh.

Gage slants back with his brows furrowed. "Are you sure? Because I'm completely cool with ditching this party and going back to my house with you."

He's such a liar. Gage loves parties.

I offer him a tight smile. "I probably never should've taken off to begin with. The parentals ... they seem nice enough."

"You sure?" He casts a wary glance at the Everettson brothers.

Easton rolls his eyes. "Stop looking at us like we're going to hurt her."

"I would if I actually believed you wouldn't." Gage's expression hardens as his eyes glide toward Foster. "From what I've seen so far, you have and you will." He protectively tugs me closer to his side.

Foster grinds his teeth with his fists balled up, his gaze locked on where Gage's side is pressed against mine.

"We're not going to hurt anyone." Easton glances at Foster before reaching forward and wrapping his fingers around my wrist. "But we do need to take this lovely thing home before our parents freak out more than they already are."

I begrudgingly wiggle my arm from Easton's grip then turn back to Gage. "I'm sorry I'm ditching out early. Tell Nina I'm sorry, too."

He gapes at me. "You're seriously leaving?"

I understand his confusion, since we've all spent the last few years doing whatever the hell we want whenever we want. But things are different now. The thunder booming outside and the heat in my chest makes me all too aware of that.

"I'll text you later, okay?" I tell Gage apologetically.

The Everettsons move to leave, and I follow, walking backward and giving Gage a slight wave.

He frowns. "See ya later then, I guess."

I wish I could tell him more—tell him everything—but even if the wall is down, I don't think it's a possibility right now. Maybe when I learn more about my new world and my powers, then I can stop being such a liar.

But from all the warnings everyone has given me so far, I'm betting I may just have to spend the rest of my life lying to everyone I care about.

CHAPTER 18

I GRAB MY BAG BEFORE WE LEAVE AND HEAD OUT into the crowded living room. No one says goodbye to me, but that's basically the story of my life. I do, however, notice several girls checking out Max, Eaton, and Foster. Max and Foster either don't care or are oblivious to the attention. Easton soaks it up, though, winking and dazzling them with smiles.

When I roll my eyes, he offers me the same grin, to which I roll my eyes again.

"You know, if you keep doing that, your eyes are going to get stuck like that," Easton teases. "And I seriously think that might depress Foster."

I make a big show of crossing my eyes, and Easton chuckles.

Foster scowls at Easton. "Knock it off."

Easton gives him an innocent look. "Knock what off?"

"You know what," Foster murmurs, yanking open the front door.

Grinning, Easton steps outside, and the rest of us follow.

An overcast covers the sky, and a light drizzle of rain trickles down from the clouds.

Easton gives an insinuating glance at Foster and me, and then a devious grin rises on his lips. "All right, which one of you is doing this?"

I crinkle my nose. "I don't think it's me ... I'm too high right now."

Easton cocks a brow. "You know my parents aren't going to be cool with that, right?"

"Yeah, I got that impression yesterday." I tuck a strand of rain-damped hair behind my ear as we slowly make our way across the puddled grass. "I'm not really used to that sort of stuff."

"What stuff?" Max asks, rain trickling across his face.

"Parents being"—I shrug—"strict, I guess."

"So, your parents just let you get high?" Max asks with his brows puckered.

I nod, and he trades a glance with Easton and Foster. All of their expressions may be unreadable, but I have a pretty good gist of what they're thinking.

"My parents were—are decent parents," I protest. "They're just... chill. There's nothing wrong with that."

They share another glance, and then Easton blows out a sigh.

"Well, chill or not," he says to me, "you're still going to have to sober up a bit before we get home or they're going to be even more upset than they already are."

"She's going to have to get rid of her bloodshot eyes, too." Max splashes his boots through puddles as we step onto the sidewalk in front of Nina's house. Cars are parked along the curb and in the driveway, evidence of a party, yet it's the kind of neighborhood where no one really cares. "Fost, you still have those eye drops in your glove box?"

Foster nods, stuffing his hands in his pockets. He's been really quiet since we exited the house, and I'm not sure why. Just like I'm not sure why I even care if he's quiet or why I'm aware of it.

I really need to stop fixating on him.

"Why do you have eye drops in your car? Do you smoke, too?" I ask as Foster, Easton, and Max slow to a stop beside a car.

I halt with them, realizing they drove Foster's Chevelle. Memories of the last time I was near it flash through my mind, and I internally grimace.

Well, sort of. I honestly feel a bit dazed from the few hits I took.

Foster gives me a funny look as he glances at my face. "No ... They're not human eye drops we're talking about."

"So, they're magical eye drops?" It sounds so funny talking about magic aloud.

I'm uncertain what sort of face I pull, but Foster smashes his lips together, biting back an amused smile. "Yeah, they are."

"What do they do?" My eyelashes flutter as the rain picks up and raindrops splatter across my face.

"They change the color of my eyes." He digs out his car keys, unlocks the passenger door, then steps back and lets Max climb into the back.

"Why do you need to change your eye color?" I shield my eyes from the rain with my hand.

He scuffs the tip of his boot against the wet concrete, his gaze lowering to the ground. "To hide what I am when I need to."

My lips form an O. "So, does that mean I'm going to have to use the eye drops, too?"

He lifts his gaze to mine and nods. "Whatever eye color you choose is the only power you'll pretend to have, which means you'll only be able to use that power when you're around others."

I pretend like I understand but, deep down, I'm

still so confused. "What power do you pretend to only have?"

He nods at Easton. "I went with silver—water—like Easton, since we're twins."

"But I can pick whatever one I want, right?" Because if I can, I'm not choosing water.

"I guess so ... But ..." He doesn't finish, trading another look with Easton.

Tired of their secret looks, I move to get in the back with Max, when Easton jumps in front of me.

"You can sit up front." He ducks his head to get in.

Out of the three of them, Max has been the nicest to me, so ...

"I'm cool with sitting in the back," I say then move to swing around him and get in, but he sidesteps, blocking my path.

His gaze briefly strays to Foster before returning to me. "Just sit in the front, okay?"

I'm pretty sure my lip juts out, which elicits chuckles from Easton and Foster.

"I promise I don't bite," Foster says, stepping closer to me and lightly tracing his finger along the inside of my wrist.

Light sparks tickle across my skin, a streak of blue zaps across the sky, and the rain picks up even more.

Rolling his eyes, Easton slides into the back seat with Max. "His flirting skills suck," he whispers to

Max. "I think we really might need to give him some lessons."

Foster lets out an exhausted sigh.

I step to the side, putting some space between us then meet his intense gaze. "I don't trust you," I feel the need to say. "At all."

He forcefully smashes his lips together, and lightning blazes across the sky. "I know I said you weren't safe with us and we wouldn't protect you, but I was lying. We—I won't ever hurt you."

I lift a brow. "You mean hurt me again?" The moment the words leave my lips, I instantly regret them.

A crease forms between his brows. "When did I hurt you?"

Can he seriously not remember? Or maybe he thinks his rejection didn't affect me? If that's the case, maybe I should just play this off before I end up embarrassing myself.

"Nothing. Never mind." I move to get in the car, but he enfolds his fingers around my arm.

"No, seriously, I want to know," he says, steering me back toward him.

Great. Why did I have to open my mouth?

Probably because I'm high and not thinking very clearly.

Maybe that's why I say, "When I approached you at the auto shop, you were a dick and it hurt my feelings. And you've been a dick pretty much every time you're around me, up until you found out what I am. So, I know the only reason you're being civil to me right now is because I'm the only person—creature—whatever the heck I am—you can be in a relationship with. At least, I think that's what's going on ... I didn't hear the entire conversation." I bite down on my tongue as Foster's eyes widen.

"You heard that?" he whispers, horrified.

I lift a shoulder. "It's kind of why I took off."

His lips curve downward. "You shouldn't have found out that way."

"Well, I did, so ..." I swallow hard. "Is that why Grey passed out when he kissed me?"

Foster gives a slight nod, his gaze relentlessly dissecting me.

My heart rate quickens, and so does the intensity of the rain. "Will that happen every time someone tries to kiss me?"

He nods again, remorse and anguish flashing across his face as lightning illuminates in the sky. "And if you get too close to someone, your powers will end up killing them." His throat muscles work as he swallows hard. "It's the curse of being an elemental enchanter."

While I had my suspicions before, hearing him say it aloud makes my mind dizzy and my stomach churn.

"So, what? We just spend our existence alone?" I whisper, my voice getting drowned out by the rain. Still, he somehow manages to hear me. Perhaps because, in a way, we're part of the rain.

"Not necessarily ..." Heavy reluctance seeps from his tone.

I shake my head, backing away. "Nope. I'm not just going to be with you because you're the only person I can be with."

Thunder booms, the street starts to flood, and lampposts flicker as the wind howls.

Great. My emotions are all over the place. If I'm not careful, a storm is going to blow through and rip the town apart.

Taking a deep breath, I steady my voice. "I'm not going to be with someone who treated me like shit and who only decided to like me because I'm the only person he can be with. I'd rather be alone."

He blinks fiercely against the rain as he shuffles toward me, his breath fogging out from his lips. His nearness makes something shift inside me, and the heat in my veins decreases.

"I'm sorry I treated you like shit, but I never didn't not like you." His voice is soft despite the rising and crashing of his chest as he breathes raggedly. Around us, the rain morphs into light, fluffy snowflakes, and the water covering the street freezes, making the area one big ice skating rink. But Foster seems oblivious to the fact that either him or me—maybe both—have turned the entire town into a winter wonderland. "I just had to act that way ... with almost everyone."

Realization crackles through me like the icicles forming on the lampposts. "You have to keep your distance from people so you don't end up hurting them, don't you?" When he nods, the churning in my stomach increases. "I think I'm going to be sick." As my throat burns with vomit, I stumble away from him and toward the frosted bushes that border Nina's property, away from the light trickling from the porch and the moon, to puke my guts out in privacy.

When I'm positive I'm out of sight from everyone, I drop to my knees and start heaving out the contents inside my stomach.

How can this be? I mean, I was never Miss Social, and it's not like guys were lining up to date me, but the idea that I'll never have anyone, that I'll be entirely alone in this life, is frightening.

In the middle of my puking and sobbing and full-on pity party, I feel fingers brush against my back. I'd worry who it is, except the light sparks his touch brings gives it away.

"I know this is hard to take in," Foster says,

holding my damp and now frozen locks of hair away from my face, "but I promise it'll get easier with time."

Wiping my lips with the back of my hand, I tilt my head to the side and meet his gaze. He's kneeling in the snow beside me.

"Did time make it easier for you?" My breath puffs out in a cloud of smoke.

He gives a wavering nod. "It kind of did."

I assess him, debating whether he's lying or not. But I don't know him well enough to be able to tell.

"I'm not lying." He tosses a nervous glance over his shoulder, then looks back at me, his jittery nerves still evident. "I can prove it to you, too."

"Really?" I ask, and he nods. "Is it dangerous or something? Because you seem really squirrely."

"Squirrely?" he questions amusedly.

I shrug. "It's a word."

His amused smile breaks through, then he sticks out his hand toward me. When my hands remain at my sides, he sighs. "If you want to see if I'm lying, you have to take my hand."

Part of me doesn't want to, wants to hold a grudge against him for being such a jerk. But the other part of me is curious, so I place my palm in his.

Heat singes through my veins, making my heart rate accelerate, along with the snows downward trek.

"Are we doing that?" I whisper, glancing up at the frostbitten sky.

"Yeah ... I'm usually better at controlling my powers, but I think being this close to another elemental enchanter is making me a bit ... off." His cheeks are flushed, probably from the cold.

"How does it even work? I mean, our powers ... We get them from the elements, right? But how exactly? What makes us different from humans? And why do you have other powers as well? And do we live longer or do we have the same lifespan as humans? Are we human at all? Are we ...?" I drift off as he stares at me with wide eyes. "Sorry, that was a lot of questions all at once. I'm just ... curiously confused."

"Curiously confused," he mumbles with a trace of an amused smile.

Why he finds my verbiage so amusing is beyond me.

"Why are you smiling like that?" I wipe a few snowflakes off my head with the sleeve of my shirt. "I wasn't trying to be funny."

"I know ... You're just ... You're cute." He hastily clears his throat then encloses his hand around mine. "But to answer your questions; we're different from humans and can control elements because our bloodlines are connected to element gods and goddesses. There's a really long story behind it that I don't have time to get into right now, but I'm sure you'll learn about in history class. As for living longer, most elemental protectors live about twice as long as a human. As for us ..." He pales a bit. "Elemental enchanters have a much shorter lifespan, mostly because we're hunted."

"Oh." A shiver rolls up my spine, and not from the cold. "I guess that makes sense since we're the only two left." My voice sounds so hollow, numb, but inside, my heart is racing.

Shorter lifespan? Gods and goddesses? How is this my life now?

"That we know of," he corrects. When even more puzzlement sweeps through me, he adds, "There may be a chance that there are more around, but they've gone into hiding. Not that we have proof or anything. It's all just speculation."

"Have you ever thought about going into hiding?"

"A couple of times, and sometimes I think my parents would prefer I did. But going into hiding means either being away from my family or forcing them to leave their lives and hide with me. Neither of those are what I want to do right now. But I also have a family that has a good balance of different elements." He threads his fingers through mine. "Most families usually have the same elemental powers amongst everyone, and as far as I known, none have an elemental enchanter, so the fact that we have two fires, one wind, two ices, and two waters makes us very powerful when we're together."

"How did you guys end up with so many different types of elemental powers if it's not that common?"

"Most elemental protectors like to stick to their own kind. My family didn't, so we ended up with a bunch of different elements in our bloodlines. Our bloodlines can also be tracked back directly to not only the goddess of ice but also the god of water."

My eyes are nearly bulging out of my head. "I don't ..." I rub my forehead with the heel of my free hand. "This is a lot to take in."

"I can imagine." He squeezes my hand. "Do you want me to prove to you now that it'll get easier?"

I rub my chilled lips together as I lower my hand. "It's not going to hurt or make me pass out like I did in the living room, right?"

He shakes his snowflakes-covered head. "That was my fault ... I wasn't expecting so much power to flow between us, and I ..." He sinks his teeth into his bottom lip and takes a deep breath. "I won't let it happen again."

"Okay." Talking about me blacking out reminds me of something. "When I blacked out in the living room ... I saw ... or, well, more like heard darkness speaking to me, telling me it wanted me to be its queen

..." I expect him to flip out and call me a freak, but he just offers me an understanding look.

"It happens sometimes with our kind," he explains solemnly. "Because we have darkness inside us, it calls out, mostly in times of weakness ..." He releases a fog-laced exhale. "I'll teach you how to block it if you want me to. It's kind of complicated, but"—he scratches his cheek, his flush deepening—"if darkness is already speaking to you, you should probably learn soon. There's been some elemental enchanters over the course of our history who allowed the darkness to get to them and went insane."

I gulp. "There aren't any elemental protectors of darkness at this academy I'm going to, are there ...?" I trail off when his expression says all I need to know. "Will I be safe there?"

He nods without missing a beat. "Easton and I will make sure nothing happens to you. And after some time, when you learn how to control your powers better, you'll be able to protect yourself pretty damn well." He gives a short, considering pause. "But it's always best to stay away from the darkness elemental protectors as much as possible."

"What about humans? It's cool if I hang out with them, right? I'm assuming so since they go to your— our—school, but they also don't know you guys exist, so ... And you guys acted so weird toward me living with you when you thought I was human, so ..." I waver my head from side to side. "I'm a little confused by how that works. Not that I'd ever give up Nina and Gage, just an FYI. They're my best friends. Always have been."

He hesitates. "Most of our kind don't hang out with humans because hiding our powers from them can get complicated. As for the school, there're two buildings at the academy—one for human-related classes and one for element-related classes. So, for the most part, except for the standard classes, we aren't around humans very much."

"But, wouldn't it be easier to have a separate school? Or go attend school in your world?"

"Our world is also very overly populated, so a lot of us were sort of forced to come live here." He rubs a hand across his head, causing the snowflakes in his hair to melt. "As for going to separate schools, it'd probably be easier, but the council thinks it's better if we attend with humans, not only so we can practice keeping our powers a secret, which is very important, but it also helps us learn to live in the human world."

I sit back in the snow, the chilled air not bothering me as much as it probably should. "Isn't it going to be weird for me to start in the middle of the semester? I'm assuming there's going to be classes related to our powers, yet I know nothing about them."

"We're going to have to explain your situation—that you didn't know what you were until recently. Well, that you didn't know you were an elemental protector, which does happen sometimes, mostly when one of our kind puts up someone for adoption. And as for classes, you'll probably just stick to most of the same class you were already taking at your old school, but I think we might want to get you into a couple of basic element related classes so you can start learning about our world more." He shifts, sitting down in the snow in front of me without releasing his hold on my hand. "But no matter what happens, we can't let anyone know you're an elemental enchanter, so you're going to have to decide on which element you want to be before tomorrow so you can pretend to be that when you're around other elemental protectors."

His words make my stomach churn again. I want to pull away from him, curl up in a ball, and melt into the snow just so I don't have to deal with this, but the idea of letting go of his hand ... my fingers won't budge.

"Do you think ...? Do you guys think I was put up for adoption?" I utter quietly.

Pity floods his eyes. "I don't know, but we'll find out. In fact, I'm sure my parents are already digging into your history."

"It'd help if we could just find my parents," I mutter, tucking my free hand into the pocket of my jacket. "But I don't think that's going to happen anytime soon since the police are pretty much putting zero effort into it."

"I think my parents are planning on hiring an elf to try to track them down."

I blink. "Come again?"

He chuckles. "Elves are very good at tracking things."

"And are very real apparently," I mumble in shock. "Jesus, this is crazy. First, I find out there're elemental powers. Then you start talking about gods and goddesses and elves. And then, of course there's the faerie in your house. Which, FYI, I'm pretty sure he knows what I am."

He swallows audibly. "Yeah, we already figured that out when my mom went to check on him after you passed out in the living room."

Weight piles down on my shoulders as the severity of the situation hits me, yet I somehow feel a bit lighter. After years of keeping silent about my powers, it feels almost liberating to be speaking so openly about them. And to someone who understands it.

Of course, that doesn't make the dangerous world I've been thrown into any easier to deal with.

"I'm assuming it's a bad thing that he knows what I am, and it probably means I'm in danger, right?"

"As much danger as I'm in for him knowing what I am." He skims his finger along the back of my hand. "We can be in this together, though. You don't have to go through it alone."

As much as I like his offer, I hesitate to accept. "I don't want to sound like a bitch, but just because we're the only two left of our kind, doesn't mean we have to be friends. You didn't even like me until you knew what I was. And then, the first time we met ... well, I'm pretty sure you thought I was disgusting."

Snow lightly flutters around, the storm so calm and at ease now, despite the chill in the air. The calmness makes me wonder what kind of mood I'm in, what kind of emotions he's feeling.

"I didn't—don't think you're disgusting," he finally says. "I already told you that I keep my distance from people because I sort of have to." He points back at the house where music is booming. "If I didn't, a lot of people and creatures would end up in an even worse condition than the guy who kissed you. Not that I care about what happened to him. The asshole deserved it because you didn't want him to." His muscles tighten with tension, and the wind briefly roars, but he quickly collects himself and a stillness takes over the air again.

"Grey did deserve it and everything ... He's always been an asshole to me—most people have." I pick at my fingernails, nervous about what I'm going to say, mostly because it'll be admitting that I was kind of trying to hit on him that day. "So, your rejection was nothing new. And I get why you did it, but maybe next time a girl approaches you like that, you could turn her down without being such a douchebag."

"I'll try." He places his other hand over mine, stopping me from picking at my fingernails. "I'm sorry for being such an asshole, but I promise it wasn't because I think you're disgusting." A contemplative look crosses his face, but he swiftly erases it. "And I'm pretty sure Grey and almost every other guy doesn't find you disgusting either ... You're very ..." He dithers. "Well, you're gorgeous."

I snort. "Okay."

"Snort all you want, but every single one of my brothers has hit on you. Even Holden, and he rarely hits on anyone." He looks away, scratching his cheek. "But yeah, anyway, if I was a normal human guy or knew what you were that day when you walked up to my car, things would've gone down completely differ-ent. But unfortunately, I thought you were just a really pretty human girl that I could never date, so what was the point of even trying?"

My cheeks warm at the compliment, my body

reacting to his words. Or well, maybe my power is. But my mind isn't completely buying it. I mean, if what he's saying is true then why have guys avoided me like the plague? Not that it matters. It's not like I want guys to like me simply because I'm pretty.

"It must be lonely to live like that," I say in a desperate attempt to steer the conversation away from me. "To have to push everyone away." Not that my life has been full of people either. In fact, most of the time I feel lonely except maybe when I'm around Nina and Gage. But even then I feel like I have to put a wall up between us. "And the idea that I might have to ... I mean, am I eventually going to hurt Nina or Gage? They're my best friends, and we're really close."

"Friendships are fine, for the most part. It has more to do with if you become ... intimate with someone and get in a situation where you lose control over your emotions." His gaze collides with mine, his cheeks flushed, but I don't know if it's from either the cold or embarrassment. "Our emotions have a lot of control over our powers."

I peek up at the snowy sky. "Yeah, I've noticed." I lower my gaze back to him. "Every time I get angry or too sad, I either flood the streets or send a storm through town. I've even started a couple of fires. Thankfully, no one's gotten hurt from it."

"Did you ever consider telling your parents?"

"No. I thought if I told anyone, they'd lock me up in a psych ward or something. Of course, if I'd known they knew about elemental protectors, my life would've been a hell of a lot easier, and there'd still be a grocery store on Main and Peach Fall Lane."

He frowns. "What happened to the grocery store?"

"When I was about twelve, Grey and some of his friends where there, making fun of me loud enough for me to hear. I was really hormonal at the time." I had just started my period, but I'm not about to say that aloud. "I was so upset that I ended up starting a fire." My gaze drops to the ground as shame builds in me. "Thankfully, everyone got out, but the firefighters couldn't put the fire out in time, so the place burned to the ground." Even now, just talking about it makes me feel awful. If only I'd known about my powers all along, then the store would still be around.

He fixes a finger under my chin, forcing me to meet his gaze. "When I was six and still learning how to control my powers, I flooded my grandparents' house. It ruined the entire foundation and cost them thousands of dollars to fix. Plus, my grandma's cat died." A gradual exhale eases from his lips. "I felt awful about it. And guilty. I even cried for hours, calling myself a cat killer."

"Aw, that's so sad. You must've been a very sweet

boy." To lighten the mood, I grin. "Too bad that didn't stick."

He narrows his eyes at me, but the corners of his lips twitch. "My point is that, even with all the training I had, I still fucked up. And I still do fuck up. All elemental protectors and enchanters do at some point or another. It comes with having power. But our powers can do a lot of good things, too."

"Like what?" I ask, genuinely intrigued.

"Like protect our worlds from certain evils. Some of us can heal the sick. Some of us can stop droughts. We can create energy." He opens his free hand in front of us and sparks of blue emit from his palm. "The possibilities are endless when you really think about it, and elemental enchanters in particular have helped stop many wars over the course of history." He folds his fingers inward, smothering the light.

Snow lazily descends to the ground as I attempt to process everything he said.

"Shit," he abruptly mutters.

"What is it?" I ask as he retrieves his phone from his pocket.

He glances at the screen. "It's my mom. She's wondering if we're close to being home. She also wants to make sure we have you with us."

"Is everything okay?"

"Yeah, she's just worried about how you're handling this. Plus, she doesn't like us out this late."

"The concept of that is sort of lost on me," I admit. "I've always done what I want whenever I want."

"We kind of assumed that when we showed up to move you out of your house and you didn't bother cleaning up all the beer bottles off the floor," he says with a smile.

"Yeah, I think your dad wasn't too happy about that."

"It's not a bad thing, though, for parents to care."

I opt to say nothing, feeling like, if I did agree with him, I'd be betraying my parents. Then again, they knew about this entire world and never told me. If they did, my life would've been much simpler.

"We should probably get going." He stands up, and since he's holding my hand, I stand up with him, dusting the snow off the back of my pants. "Before we go, though, I want to show you something." His grip on my hand constricts.

"What ...?" My words fade as his eyes illuminate, casting an eerie glow around us, and bright images pierce through my thoughts. Images connected to memories, but not mine.

No, what I'm seeing are Foster's memories, bits and pieces of how he struggled to control his powers while growing up. How he used to start fires, floods, and lightning storms all the time. How he struggled with being the only one of his kind. How lonely he felt when he realized he'd never be able to get close to anyone. But as the memories drift closer to the present, his feelings and isolation begin to shift. He became more comfortable with what he is as he accepted his fate of being alone, of never being with anyone, of knowing that his power could do good one day, of—

For a flame flicker of a second, an image of me approaching his car that awful day ghosts through me, along with a tremendous amount of fear. But it hastily fades as he jerks his hand away from mine and breaks the connection between us.

"What was that?" I breathe out, the air between us electrified.

"That was one of my gifts." He slips his hands into his pockets and kicks at the snow with the tip of his boot. "I can project my thoughts and emotions to others."

"Wow." I shake my head in astonishment. "That's seriously crazy. Crazy cool, but still crazy.

"Yeah, but it's usually pretty useless."

"No way. You should use that power all the time."

He shakes his head. "Why would I want to share my feelings and thoughts with others? It's ... personal."

I rub my hands up and down my arms as the cold

air finally begins to wear on me. "Then, why did you share them with me?"

He gives a nonchalant shrug. "Because you need reassurance that things won't be so hard to deal with in the future."

"Well, thanks, I guess." I pause. "I saw the memory of when I approached you that day, and I'm trying to figure out how that helped you deal with your gift easier."

He stiffens. "Yeah, I didn't mean to show you that memory."

I want to ask him why he felt so afraid that day, but he doesn't give me the opportunity.

"We should get going," he mumbles then hurries for the car, his boots crunching the snow.

As I silently trail after him, I can almost feel the wall go up between us, whatever connection we felt in those bushes dissolving like the snow underneath my boots, leaving me to wonder what started the connection to begin with.

CHAPTER 19

"You two have fun playing hide and seek in the bushes?" Easton teases after Foster and I climb in the car.

Foster looks at me and rolls his eyes.

Despite everything that's happened, I can't help smiling at the fact that we get to share a private look instead of the other way around.

"Actually, we did," Foster replies, starting up the engine.

"It took Foster a while to find me," I play along. "And then I spent, like, five minutes trying to explain to him the concept that it was his turn to hide."

Foster smiles as he straps on his seatbelt, and I do the same.

"Aw, look at you two, being all BFFs." Easton

scoots forward and rests his arms on the console. "Makes me really wonder, though, what happened in those bushes." He waggles his eyebrows at me.

I pinch his arm in response, and Max chuckles from behind me when Easton winces.

"So vicious," Easton mutters with a smirk, sliding back in the seat.

We grow quiet as Foster pulls out onto the street, driving slow because of the ice glazing the asphalt.

"I can't believe we caused all this," I mutter as I eyeball the frosted trees around us. "Although, it does make it feel more like the holidays. You know, if we wanted to, we could probably cause a big enough snowstorm that they will have to cancel school for at least a few weeks."

Foster and Easton chuckle, while Max says observingly, "She's speaking more openly about her powers, yet that damn wall is still up around her. It makes no sense." He leans around the headrest and studies me with a crinkle at his brow. "Although, the crack is a little bit bigger now. My bet is the wall is really strong so it might take us some time and quite a few more attempts before we can get it down."

"I'm not going to pass out every time you try to get it down, am I?" I shudder, recalling how the darkness called to me when I passed out.

Foster shakes his head. "Now that I know what to

expect from your powers, I should be able to stabilize us better."

I nod in relief. "Good."

My phone buzzes from inside my bag, and I reach in to dig it out, figuring it's Nina. But as I'm pulling it out, the card that weird guy gave me falls onto my lap.

"What's that?" Foster wonders, giving a nod at the card.

"Oh." I pick up the card, noting it's still blank. "It's actually a weird story. Yesterday, when you guys moved my stuff out of my house, when I left for lunch with my friends, this guy came up to me and warned me about you guys. Said you weren't who I thought you were, and that, when I wanted to know the truth, to call him." I hold up the card. "He gave me this, but there isn't anything on it."

"Let me see it." Max takes the card from me and glances at the front and back with a worried look on his face.

"I should also probably point out that, when I accidentally made the lights flicker on and off, he glanced up, almost like he knew I had powers—" I startle as Foster and Easton let out a string of curses. "What's wrong?" I glance at them both.

Foster's grip on the wheel tightens. "Sky, this is very important. Did this guy have any strange markings on him?"

"Like tattoos," Easton adds.

I nod. "He had them all over his neck."

Foster swallows hard while Easton mutters, "Fucking hunters."

Panic flares through me, and the ground ripples, jolting the car.

"Easy, Sky." Foster reaches across the console and brushes his fingers along the back of my hand. "Nothing bad's going to happen, okay?"

While it's nice to be able to be comforted when my powers are going crazy, they look too worried for me to calm down.

I chew on my fingernail. "The guy who gave me the card ... he's a hunter?"

Foster gives a wavering nod, skimming his finger along the back of my hand again. "It sounds like it."

"And hunters are the ones who captured your dad and tried to do experiments on him?" I ask, and Foster nods again. "But, why did this hunter approach me then?"

"I'm not sure." Foster throws a glance at Max. "Can you figure out what's on that card?"

Max turns the card over in his hand. "I think it has a see-the-truth spell on it."

"What the hell is that?" I ask, twisting around in the seat to look at him.

"It's basically a spell that can only be seen through

if you want to see the truth." He hands me back the card, and I hesitantly take it. "So, I think, if you focus on wanting to see the truth, a message will appear."

I stare down at the card in my hand. "But, what truth am I even going to see?"

"The truth about whatever that hunter wanted you to see." Max gives a considering pause. "I'm guessing it's about us since he mentioned us."

"Either that or he knows about her and was trying to set a trap to catch her," Easton mutters from the back seat.

I swallow shakily. "But then, why didn't he just take me?"

"Hunters are weak when it comes to powers," Easton says. "If you really wanted to, you could probably take down at least a dozen of them simply by calling out to the sky."

"Yeah, but I didn't know that at the time he gave me the card," I point out.

"Maybe he didn't know that, though," Easton says. "Of course, if you can see past the spell on that card, we might have the answer."

I glance down at the card again. "If hunters aren't powerful, then how did this guy put a spell on the card?"

Easton dismisses me with a flick of his wrist.

"That's merely a party trick. Almost anyone can do that."

"Anyone can do magic?" I ask in disbelief.

He lifts a shoulder. "Party trick magic, sure. You just need the right ingredients."

"So, hunters are human?" I ask, trying to make sure I'm following.

Easton wavers. "It all depends on if you believe humans without souls are still human."

I gape at him. "They don't have souls?"

Easton gives an uneven nod. "They trade their souls in order to work for the labs."

"But, what do they get out of it?" I wonder, my heart thudding in my chest. "And why do they have to give up their souls?"

"No one's really sure," Max answers. "But my dad has a theory that the labs are trying to extract the powers out of elementals, so maybe the hunters get promised those powers. He's not sure why they have to give up their souls, though, other than maybe they won't have a conscience and will be okay with what they do."

When I shiver, Foster reaches out to crank up the heat.

"You're fine," he says. "No one's going to get ahold of you."

If that's even what the hunters want. When the guy approached me in the diner, it seemed as if he was trying to warn me of the Everettsons, not take me to some lab.

Deciding to find out the answer, I let my gaze burn into the card while trying to focus on seeing past the magic, seeing the truth. And after a minute or two passes, words begin to appear. I read them to myself then aloud.

"If you're reading this note, I'm sure you've noticed by now that the Everettson family isn't your ordinary family. If you'd like answers and someone to talk to, please contact me at the following number. Whatever you tell me about them, I won't think you're crazy. I understand that strange things exist, more than most people do."

"Let me see that." Max takes the card from me, reads it over, then swallows hard. "It sounds like they're trying to use Sky to get information on us."

"How did they even find out she was moving in with us?" Easton questions then gives me an accusing look. "Have you been talking to people about us?"

I scowl at him. "Who the fuck would I tell? I have, like, two friends. And besides, up until you showed up on my doorstep, I didn't even realize I'd be living with a family of eight. All I knew was your last name. I

didn't even realize Foster was an Everettson when I ..."
I bite down on my lip before I say something that is
definitely going to embarrass me.

But maybe Foster already told everyone about
when I tried to hit on him?

"When you what?" Easton presses with intrigue.

"Nothing." I sneak a look in Foster's direction,
only to find him focusing solely on the road.

Huh. Now I'm pretty sure he didn't tell them.
That's a surprise, but one I'm relieved about.

"It still doesn't make sense that they targeted you,"
Max mumbles distractedly. "Unless they've been
watching you for a while. But hunters don't usually
watch humans, so maybe they know what you are."

"If that's the case, why aren't they trying harder to
get to her? And her wall makes it really complicated to
see what she really is," Foster points out, but worry
rings in his tone. "My bet is they found out she was
moving in with us and are trying to recruit her into
helping them."

Unsettling silence passes between them.

"I think we need to do something about this," Max
says with an edge in his tone.

The tension in the air crushes against my lungs,
and I nearly dive out of the car. I would have if we
weren't driving. If I tried now, I'd probably hurt myself

pretty badly. Then again, from what I've learned about the Everettsons, they'll do a lot to keep their family secrets a secret, which leaves me a bit worried that maybe I'll get hurt no matter what.

CHAPTER 20

I don't jump out of the car. I want to. Fuck, do I want to. But as the storm picks up, probably because of the worry seeping out between Foster and me, I decide against it.

No one says much of anything for the rest of the drive home. Although, I do notice everyone gives edgy glances at the forest lining the road, as if they expect a bunch of hunters to jump out at any minute. Fortunately, that never happens and we make it home safely.

Before we head inside, Foster digs a small vial filled with a clear, glittery liquid from out of the glove box. The eye changing drops, I'm assuming.

"Put a couple of drops of this in each of your eyes while thinking about your eyes being less bloodshot, and it should clear the red out of it," he says, handing me the vial.

"Okay." But I make no effort to do so.

"It won't hurt," Foster promises. "It just feels sort of sparkly."

"It's not pain I'm worried about." I scratch my eye. "I just don't like putting things in my eyes."

Foster rubs his lips together. "You want me to help you?"

I nod eagerly. "Yes, please." I give him back the vial.

He pats the console. "Rest your head on this and try to keep your eyes open, okay?"

I obey, resting my head on the console. But as soon as he positions the vial over my eye, I start blinking like crazy.

"Try not to blink, okay?" He waits for me to nod then moves the vial over my eye again.

I blink.

He sighs, but a trace of an amused smile tugs at his lips. "Okay, I'm going to have East hold your eye open."

I pull a face but don't argue.

Easton grins as he leans over me, reaching for my eye.

"I have a feeling you're enjoying this way too much," I remark as Easton holds my eye open.

His grin broadens. "Now, why would you think that?" Then he moves his fingers closer together, making my eye close then open again. "Look, she's winking at me."

"Good gods, East, you can be so annoying sometimes." Max nudges him out of the way and offers me an apologetic look before holding my eye open.

Foster hurries and applies the drops in one eye then the other before sitting back and putting the cap back on the vial.

I sit up, blinking, my eyeballs feeling weirdly sparkly. "This feels so weird."

Foster scans my face over, his gaze lingering on my eyes. "Your eyes aren't red anymore, though."

I pull the visor down and look at my reflection in the mirror. Sure enough, my eyes are completely bloodshot free. "Man, if Gage knew this shit existed, he'd be all over it."

A muscle in Foster's jaw ticks. "Gage, your friend, right?"

I nod, giving him a perplexed look. "Yeah, the guy you met just barely." Not that I believe he's forgotten who Gage is. I just don't understand why he's double-checking.

Nodding, Foster climbs out of the car, while Easton snickers and Max sighs.

Sighing myself, I hop out of the car and follow

Foster out the garage and up the path to the front door of the house.

"So, how much trouble am I going to be in?" I ask Foster as we enter the foyer.

"Well, since it's your first offense, not too much." He aims for a teasing tone but misses the mark. "Honestly, after we tell my parents that a hunter has contacted you, I think they're probably going to forget about you taking off tonight."

"Good. Well, I don't mean that it's good a hunter contacted me, but I'm glad I'm probably not going to get in too much trouble tonight," I nervously ramble.

A ghost of a smile touches his lips, but then it fades as he frowns. "They're still going to have to do something about the hunter being in contact with you. They need to make sure our family's secrets stay secret."

Nervousness creeps through me, but before I can ask what his parents are going to do to me, Emaline appears at the top of the stairs.

"Oh, thank gods you're back." She hurries down the stairs and rushes up to me, wrapping her arms around me.

So not the reaction I was expecting, but I awkwardly hug her back anyway.

"I'm so sorry we freaked you out, but you can

never run off like that again, okay?" She pulls back and waits for me to answer, but Foster speaks first.

"Actually, she had a good reason to take off." He massages the back of his neck tensely, staring at the floor. "She overheard us talking about what it means to be an elemental enchanter, particularly about how I—we can't be with anyone else..." He trails off, scratching his cheek and looking away

"Oh." Her expression plummets as she stares at me with concern. "I'm so sorry you had to find out that way. We were going to tell you, but ..."

"It's a lot to take in." Foster briefly meets my gaze, his pupils sparking. Then he blinks and looks at Emaline. "Mom, you don't have to worry. I explained a lot of it to her."

Emaline's brows rise in surprise, but then a knowing smile pulls at her lips. That smile dissipates, though, when Easton and Max enter the house and Max announces, "A hunter has been in contact with her."

More fear than I've ever seen in anyone's face consumes Emaline's expression, and suddenly, I find myself wishing I'd chosen to dive out of the car when I had the chance.

CHAPTER 21

"So, what are we going to do?" Holden asks, glancing apprehensively at Gabe.

After Emaline found out a hunter had been in contact with me, all the Everettsons and I piled into the living room so we could discuss what happened. By the time Max, Easton, Foster, and I finished explaining the card and how a hunter approached me, fear had swept across everyone's faces. I felt afraid, too, but mostly over what they're going to do with me.

I'm nervous. I'm not going to lie. I wish I'd taken a seat closer to the exit. You know so I can take off if I need to. Instead, I'm sitting on the sofa in the center of the room. Max and Porter are beside me, Foster, Easton, and Hunter are seated on the sofa across from me, Holden is perched on the coffee table close to the doorway, and Emaline and Gabe are seated in chairs beside the fireplace where a fire is crackling, remnants of the portal no longer evident.

"We'll continue to do what we've been doing," Gabe answers Holden after a quietness haunts the room for an unnerving amount of time. "We'll keep our walls up around us and the protection spells around the house and yard. We can also retouch the protection spells on everyone, and make sure our powers are at full strength, which means extra practice sessions."

Another drop of silence skips by, and it's hard not to be aware of how shifty everyone has gotten. No one is directly making eye contact with me, either staring at the fire, the doorway, or each other. Honestly, hardly anyone has said anything to me at this point, but I guess that's typical. Well, it was up until yesterday when I moved in with them. They've paid more attention to me than anyone has in a long time. I'm not sure how I feel about that, just like I'm unsure how I feel about their lack of attention now.

"What about Sky?" Holden breaks the silence, avoiding my questioning gaze and looking directly at Gabe. "She's ... Well, she's weak controlling her powers, and it'll take her years to be able to get them to full strength."

Shock courses through me, and I cringe as the

lights flicker on and off, announcing my hurt. But, out of all of them, Holden seemed like the nicest. Then again, he's only saying the truth. The truth sort of hurts like a bitch, though.

"I can go back to live in Honeyton," I offer quietly, folding my arms around myself. "I'm sure I can crash with Nina or Gage, just as long as you guys don't report me as a runaway or anything."

Emaline shakes her head but doesn't utter a word, looking at Gabe. Their silent exchange goes on for an unsettling amount of time, and everyone begins to grow fidgety.

I'm not going to lie. It hurts when no one protests for me to stay. But it's fine. I'm fine. I'm always fine.

You're such a liar.

When my heart starts to do weird things, I decide it's time to say *peace out* and go pack my shit.

Sucking in a breath, I push to my feet and step toward the doorway.

"Where are you going?" Max jumps up in front of me and snags ahold of my arm.

In the blink of an eye, all of them are standing up.

Panic rushes through me, making my heart pound and the house rattle as spurts of lightning vibrate from outside.

Emaline glances at the chandelier clinking above our heads, then her gaze lands on me. "Sky, sweetie, I know this situation is scary, but you need to calm down."

"I'm trying." But, as they all take a step toward me, my adrenaline soars and lightning streaks across the ceiling and thunder booms from inside, shaking everything.

"Holy shit," Porter murmurs, looking from the ceiling to me. "Oh honey, you've got some wicked power in you." The lightning lights up the delight in his eyes.

Delight that I don't understand.

I gulp, looking around at the eight of them. All of them have their eyes fixed on me. But it's not comforting. In fact, I think it might be worse than when they wouldn't look at me.

"Look, I promise I won't tell anyone any of your secrets. Honestly, I don't really know a lot of your secrets, other than what everyone is, but I swear I won't say a word," I ramble, loathing the trembling in my tone. "Just please don't hurt me."

Max's brows pull together. "Hurt you?" He glances at Emaline, whose eyes are wide with horror.

"Sweetie, we're not going to hurt you." She steps toward me and takes my hands in hers. "We're just trying to decide something."

"Something that might need to be done, not only

to protect our family and our secrets," Gabe adds, "but to protect you as well."

"Oh." Okay, now I just feel stupid, but the feeling isn't new to me. "You just all seemed so nervous, and I thought you guys might ..." I stop myself, feeling awful for having the thoughts I was having.

"You thought what?" Easton asks, his lips quirking. "Come on; finish that sentence, because I'm dying to know what you think about us."

"I think she thought we were going to kill her." Hunter appears way too amused by the fact.

"No," I lie. "I just thought you might ... I don't know." I sit back down, feeling like an idiot. "I'm just a little freaked out. I'm sorry." It probably doesn't help that not all the alcohol and weed has worn out of my system and my head feels a bit foggy.

Easton snickers. "Well, at least she's entertaining."

That gets everyone to crack a smile. Even Foster. Although, he's been smiling more by the hour. But I'm trying not to focus on the reason for that.

I clear my throat as my cheeks start to warm. "So, what's this thing you guys think might need to be done? Because it seems like you're a bit hesitant about it."

"We are," Emaline says. "Not because it's dangerous. It's just very ... permanent."

They sink into silence again as they sit back down.

"I think we should do it," Hunter utters, staring down at the backs of his hands. "If she's going to be living with us for the next six months, and a hunter has been in contact with her, it's the best way not only to keep her from being on their radar, but it'll also give us peace of mind that our secrets won't get out."

"But it can't be undone," Holden reminds him. "You can't unmerge a merging enchantment."

"Merging enchantment?" I scrunch my nose. "That sounds very ... merge-y."

Foster snorts a laugh.

"Stop laughing at my words," I protest, though I can't help smiling.

"I will when your words stop being amusing," Foster quips with a grin.

"Well, aren't you two just utterly adorable," Hunter remarks with a devious smirk.

Easton snickers, and then they fist bump.

Talk about two peas in a pod, or I guess two element protectors in an overly crowded living room.

Shaking his head, Foster lightly punches Hunter's arm. "Shut the hell up, man."

Hunter shakes his head, his eyes glinting wickedly. "Payback's a bitch, little bro."

"All right, that's enough." Gabe claps his hands and rises to his feet again. "Everettsons, we need to make a choice. Either you can do a merging enchantment with Sky, or we can take the risk and simply keep an extra eye on her. If we choose the latter, we can do shifts so she's never alone, and we'll have to try to go to Spellbinding world so we can get a few protection spells cast on her. But with what she is, we'll have to be careful taking her to other worlds without her being merged to us due to the danger." Tension pours off him as he shifts his weight and rubs the back of his neck. "Or you can choose the first one and ... Well, you guys know how that works."

"But Sky doesn't," Hunter points out. "She should probably be told first before we even consider going there, because it's a big decision for everyone."

Okay, seriously, what's the big deal with this merging enchantment?

"Yeah, you're probably right," Gabe says with a sigh. "How about this? All of you go discuss this in the kitchen while me and your mother explain things to Sky. Then we'll regroup and make a decision."

They all nod in agreement then get to their feet, filing out of the room.

The second they're all gone, Gabe lets out a deafening breath and slumps onto his chair. "I love our kids to death, but sometimes dealing with the six of them can be overwhelming," he murmurs, causing Emaline to smile, but her smile falters when she looks at me, worry taking over her face.

"I'm so sorry about this." She gets up and sits down beside me. "I'm sure you're probably beyond confused at this point."

I give a nod. "A little bit, but that's okay."

She smiles at me. "You're a very understanding girl."

"You think that, even though I took off tonight?" I wonder skeptically.

"If I overheard what you did, I would've done the exact same thing when I was your age," she tells me. "But I probably wouldn't have taken the time to text my mom and tell her I took off. Thank you for doing that, by the way. I just hope that, the next time you get scared like that, you'll stay and talk to me instead of running off."

I nod, even though nervousness pulsates through me. Next time? Just how many times am I going to get scared?

As if reading the worry on my face, she says, "We need to explain this merging enchantment to you, and I need you to try not to panic, okay? Because it might be the best choice in this situation, even if it seems a bit extreme."

I nod again, but holy hell am I freaking out. "Okay, I can do that."

"Good." She looks at Gabe then returns her attention back to me. "Our family has a lot of secrets—

important secrets—which I'm sure you've figured out by now. And it's important that the hunters don't find out. And not just about our secrets, but about Foster. Because, if they do find out about him—find out he's an elemental enchanter—they will try to use his power for terrible things."

"Which is why, a long time ago, we put a merging enchantment on all our boys." Gabe slides forward in his chair and rests his arms on his knees. "So we can protect, not only Foster, but all of them from the harshness of this world and of other worlds."

"Okay." I anxiously bite my lip. "So, what exactly is a merging enchantment?"

Emaline glances at Gabe again before looking back at me. "It's a spell that links them with each other, so they're all very in tune with one another." Emaline explains. "It bonds them so they can feel when one of them is in trouble, when they need help—stuff like that, And it swears them to secrecy so they all have to keep each other's secrets."

"The enchantment is permanent, though," Gabe stresses. "You need to understand that. If all of you choose to do it, you'll forever be linked to each other."

I gulp. "That's ..." *Well, there are no words.*

"It's a lot to take in," Emaline agrees, making me wonder if I said my thoughts aloud. "And there are other ways to protect you ..." She trails off, and I sense a *but*.

"But," Gabe finishes for her, "a merging enchantment would be the most discreet and best way to not only protect you but protect our boys."

"I don't want to scare you," Emaline says warily, "but being an elemental enchanter can be very dangerous. And if a hunter has already contacted you ..." She shakes her head, sadness masking her expression.

I'm still not fully sure I understand what a merging enchantment is in the literal sense, but I understand enough to get the basic gist of it—that it'll protect me and protect the Everettsons, and that it'll also make me connected to them forever.

"It's not like I have to be around them all the time, is it?" I double-check. "I mean, I can go places by myself ...? And eventually, when I get older, I can go on and live my life? I'll just sense them sometimes if there's a problem."

Emaline hesitantly nods. "But you'll always feel that connection to them."

"How strong of a connection?" I wonder.

"It's not extremely intense." Max appears in the doorway with his hands stuffed in his pockets. "But it's noticeable and can get kind of obnoxious when Easton is being a drama queen and thinks he needs help with everything."

"Bro, that's so not me." Easton steps up beside him and rolls his eyes. "I'm as chill as a vampire."

Vampire? My eyes widen, but no one seems to notice, as if this is all normal. But it probably is to them.

Max shakes his head. "You're about as chill as a goddamn pixie jacked up on faerie dust."

Easton's lips part with a comeback, but he trails off when Holden pushes past him, Hunter, Foster, and Porter following. All of them glance at me, yet their expressions are unreadable. Instead of sitting on the sofas, they form a small circle around the room then trade an undecipherable look with each other. No one says anything, though, and finally Easton rolls his eyes.

"Fine, I guess I'll be the spokesperson." He steps forward and dramatically clears his throat. "We discussed things and decided that, while it's going to be a little weird having a girl in our inner circle, it's probably best if we do the merging enchantment." His lips spread into a smirk as he looks directly at me. "Just as long as she doesn't send an emergency signal through the link every time she sees a mouse or gets a pimple or stupid girlie shit like that."

My lips twitch. "Oh, fuck off. I'm sure you're probably just saying that because you do that crap all the time."

His eyes sparkle in delight. "Only when I'm

having a really bad hair day. Sometimes it can get complicated looking this fantastic."

"He's not kidding," Foster says with a hint of a smile. "He spends, like, two hours in the bathroom every morning."

Easton glares at him, but the corners of his lips tug upward. "Good to know you become a traitor when you're trying to impress her."

Foster grits his teeth. "I do not."

"All right," Gabe intervenes. "Let's stop over-whelming Sky."

"Yeah right. Look at her." Easton smirks at me. "She's totally getting off on this."

I narrow my eyes and flip him the middle finger, but he only laughs.

Emaline sighs. "Good gods, sometimes I question how I've managed to stay sane all these years."

"Who says you still are?" Gabe mumbles then pulls a *whoopsie* face when she glares at him.

But then she smiles and kisses his cheek. "It's a good thing you love crazy."

I have to admit, as strange as they are, watching them interact helps me feel a bit more at ease. Of course, when they all look at me expectantly, waiting for me to agree to do the merging enchantment, all that ease fizzles.

"So, what do you say, Sky?" Easton asks with a

smirk. "You think you have the guts to do the spell or what?"

Maybe it's the smirk or the challenge in his tone. Or perhaps I'm still high and drunk and not thinking clearly. Or maybe, deep down, all the years of having to deal with my powers alone has finally gotten to me. Maybe I secretly crave having some sort of connection.

Or maybe I've just lost my damn mind.

Who the hell knows?

Whatever the reason, I find myself nodding.

"All right, yeah, let's do it," I say, hoping I'm not making a big mistake.

They all nod, but some of them appear a bit tense.

"We should probably warn you that you might pass out," Foster says. "I know you don't like that."

"No, I don't." I internally shudder as I remember passing out earlier and darkness crawling into the crevasses of my mind. "Can you, like, try to wake me up as soon as possible?"

He nods. "I'll do my best."

"Okay." I release an unsteady breath. "So, what do I have to do?"

"We stand in a circle and place our hands in each other's," Holden explains, sticking his hands out to his sides.

The others follow while Emaline and Gabe back up

at bit. That makes my nerves go up a notch. My anxiety only doubles as I place my hand in Max's, who's standing on my right, and then in Foster's, who moved to my left.

"Now what?" I ask, glancing at the six of them.

"Now close your eyes," Foster instructs, threading his fingers through mine.

As I lower my eyelids, I have the strangest thought that maybe this is all a prank. After all, Emaline said her boys like to do that sort of stuff. Then again, I doubt her and Gabe would play along.

Then, all my doubts go *bye-bye, see ya later* when a sudden wave of power blazes through me.

I gasp as I feel all their powers connect and merge with mine. Suddenly, I can feel everything they're feeling. It's brief and happens so quickly, but I have to say, some of the shit that's going on with them is a bit … complicated to deal with.

I don't get too stressed out over it, though, because a split-second later, I hear a loud *zap*, and then I pass out.

"Skylin, can you hear me?" darkness purrs in my ears.

"Go away!" I scream. "Leave me alone!"

"Now, why would we do that?" darkness whispers. "Why would we ignore our queen?"

"I'm not your queen," I whisper. "Just go away."

"We're never going away. We've waited a long time for you, and we're not going to stop until you're ours."

The voice is deep and familiar, but I can't place from where.

"Who are you?" I whisper.

"I think you should be asking: who are you ...?"

"Sky, open your eyes." Foster's voice cuts through the darkness like a zap of lightning. "Come on; wake up."

"This isn't over yet," darkness warns. "I'll be back for you, our queen of darkness."

I force my eyelids open, sucking in a sharp breath.

"Easy," Foster whispers as he strokes his fingers up and down my back.

I blink profusely as I peer around, noting I'm in my bedroom, the lights are on, and I'm lying in bed, on my side. Foster is sitting beside me on the edge of the bed with his hand on my back, and he's wearing a pair of plaid pajama bottoms and a black T-shirt.

"How long have I been out?" I sit up, rubbing my eyes.

"A couple of hours." He watches me guardedly. "I

came to check on you a couple of times, but you were pretty out of it."

"Oh." I'm touched he kept his word and tried to wake me up, but what happened while I was asleep has me distracted. "I dreamt of darkness again. It was really pushy, saying... I'm its queen." I shudder at the memory of how delighted darkness sounded about it.

He considers something while cracking his knuckles against the sides of his legs. "When I was about ten, darkness started really trying to take over my dreams. I think because my powers were developing faster and I was having a hard time controlling them."

"Did it ever call you its queen?" I ask then shake my head at myself. "Never mind. Please forget I asked that."

He smiles then scoots closer to me, bringing his legs up onto my bed. "Remember what I said in the bushes? It'll get easier with time, and the dreams will eventually go away when you learn to block the darkness out."

"I'll try to hold on to that, but I'm not going to lie, it makes me not want to go to sleep."

"You should probably try, though." He glances at the alarm clock on the nightstand. "We have to get up for school in only a couple hours."

"Shit," I murmur, flopping back on the pillow. I

stare up at the ceiling, trying to process everything that's happened and everything to come. "I'm nervous about school," I admit. "I've never been good at making friends, and now I have to try to make them in a school full of people with powers."

"You won't be totally alone," he promises. "East and I will be there."

"Yeah, but I'm sure you guys have your own lives and your own friends."

"We have a few, but not a ton. And we'll take care of you." He lies down beside me and turns his head toward me, a teasing smile playing at his lips. "If we don't, then we'll be stuck feeling your social awkwardness all day, and we definitely don't want to have to deal with that."

I playful scowl at him. "Like you guys are any better? I may have only felt what you were feeling for, like, two seconds, but there was some weird shit going on. Honestly, I may not have agreed to do the how merging thing if I knew I was going to feel everyone's internal drama."

"It won't always be as intense as when we did the merging spell. It just took a lot of strain on our power, so we couldn't control what we sent out to each other very well. But it's not always like that." He muses over something. "My bet, though, is that weird shit you felt came from Porter. I love him and everything, but he's into some weird stuff."

A smile quirks at my lips. "I think it totally was him." I roll to my side, tucking my hands underneath my cheek. My gaze skims his profile, his full lips, his lightning-blue eyes that are lined with dark, thick eyelashes.

God, he's so pretty. No wonder I had a crush on him without even seeing him close up.

He glances at me, amusement dancing in his eyes. "What?"

"Nothing." Shit, did I send my feelings to him?

Either I didn't or he lets me off the hook as he silently stares up at the ceiling again.

"Are you going to sleep in here?" I wonder when he makes no move to leave.

He casts a glance at me. "I was going to until you fell asleep, unless you want me to leave."

Part of me does. Part of me doesn't.

All of me is confused.

Maybe that's why I say, "Yeah, sure. Stay. But if you hear me murmuring in my sleep about darkness, promise you'll wake me up."

He nods, then tentatively, he reaches out and tucks a strand of hair behind my ear. "I promise I will."

My stomach flutters. Actually fucking flutters like I ate a bunch of butterflies or something, which is really gross when I think about it. Eating butterflies, I mean. And makes me very stupid for reacting to his touch this way.

What is wrong with me? Since when do I get fluttery over guys?

"Okay." I swallow, and in the silence of the room, it's noticeable.

But Foster says nothing, simply staring at me, his eyes searching mine.

"We should probably turn off the lights," I finally suggest when his gaze starts making my skin warm.

I start to sit up to do just that, but he captures my hand and pulls me back down to the bed.

"You want to know something awesome about our powers? We don't have to do mundane things like turn off lights or take forever to move stuff out of a house."

"I knew you guys didn't do that on your own." I lightly swat his arm, and he chuckles.

"Yeah, but it was so much faster, wasn't it?" he says with a smile.

"Yeah, but it still doesn't explain how you did it."

He grins. "A portal that led from your house to the storage unit. My dad created it after you left."

I shake my head in astonishment. "I don't even know what to say."

"How about *lights out?*" he suggests, giving my hand a squeeze.

I'm not sure what he's about to do, but I play along anyway. "Lights out—"

Sparks hiss between our palms, and then the light suddenly burns out.

"Okay, that was kind of cool," I admit. "Although, the pitch black is a bit unnerv—"

Before I can finish, an orb of blue, miniature lightning bolts forms in his hand.

"Okay, now you're just showing off," I say with a smile.

"Maybe just a little bit." He pivots on his side, keeping his hand glowing. "Go to sleep, Sky. You're safe from the darkness. I promise."

I wish he was right, but the second I start to close my eyes, darkness whispers to me.

All I can do, though, is hope that, in time, I'll be able to block them out.

ABOUT THE AUTHOR

Jessica Sorensen is a *New York Times* and *USA Today* bestselling author who lives in the snowy mountains of Wyoming. When she's not writing, she spends her time reading and hanging out with her family.

Enchanted Chaos Series:

Enchanted Chaos

Shimmering Chaos

Iridescent Chaos (coming soon)

Chasing Hadley Series:

Chasing Hadley

Falling for Hadley

Holding onto Hadley

Holding onto Hadley: The Deal

Untitled (coming soon)

The Breathing Undead Series

Breathing Lies

Shadowed Whisperers (coming 2019)

My Cursed Superhero Life:

Grim

Untitled (coming soon)

Capturing Magic:

Chasing Wishes

Chasing Magic

Untitled (coming soon)

Cursed Hadley:

Cursed Hadley

Enchanting Hadley (coming soon)

Tangled Realms:

Forever Violet

Untitled (coming soon)

Curse of the Vampire Queen:

Tempting Raven

Enchanting Raven

Alluring Raven

Untitled (coming soon)

Unraveling You Series:

Unraveling You

Raveling You

Awakening You

Inspiring You

Fated by Darkness
Untitled (coming soon)

Unexpected Series:

The Unexpected Way of Falling

The Unpredictable Way of Falling

Untitled (coming soon)

Shadow Cove Series:

What Lies in the Darkness

What Lies in the Dark

Untitled (coming soon)

Mystic Willow Bay Series:

The Secret Life of a Witch

Broken Magic

Untitled (coming soon)

Standalones:

The Forgotten Girl

The Illusion of Annabella

Confessions of a Kleptomaniac

Rules of a Rebel and a Shy Girl

The Heartbreaker Society:

The Opposite of Ordinary

Untitled (coming soon)

Broken City Series:

Nameless

Forsaken

Oblivion

Forbidden (coming soon)

Guardian Academy Series:

Entranced

Entangled

Enchanted

Entice (coming soon)

Sunnyvale Series:

The Year I Became Isabella Anders

The Year of Falling in Love

The Year of Second Chances

The Coincidence Series:

The Coincidence of Callie and Kayden

The Redemption of Callie and Kayden

The Destiny of Violet and Luke

The Probability of Violet and Luke

The Certainty of Violet and Luke

The Resolution of Callie and Kayden

Seth & Greyson

The Secret Series:

The Prelude of Ella and Micha

The Secret of Ella and Micha

The Forever of Ella and Micha

The Temptation of Lila and Ethan

The Ever After of Ella and Micha

Lila and Ethan: Forever and Always

Ella and Micha: Infinitely and Always

The Shattered Promises Series:

Shattered Promises

Fractured Souls

Unbroken

Broken Visions

Scattered Ashes

Breaking Nova Series:

Breaking Nova

Saving Quinton

Delilah: The Making of Red

Nova and Quinton: No Regrets

Tristan: Finding Hope

Wreck Me

Ruin Me

The Fallen Star Series:

The Fallen Star

The Underworld

The Vision

The Promise

The Lost Soul

The Evanescence

The Darkness Falls Series:

Darkness Falls

Darkness Breaks

Darkness Fades

The Death Collectors Series (NA and YA):

Ember X and Ember

Cinder X and Cinder

Spark X and Spark

Unbeautiful Series:

Unbeautiful

Untamed